OF MICE and WOLFMEN

by
Joe Pasquale

A HellBound Books Publishing LLC Book
Houston TX

Contents

Forward by Bradley Walsh

I first met Joe in the early 80's. Like a lot of young hopefuls, we had entered a talent competition at the Rolls Royce Social Club. I had been working there as an apprentice. Over the years, our paths crossed multiple times; we would be performing at various shows, clubs, and competitions.

In those early years, I never knew where he was coming from. I wasn't sure if he was putting on that persona, or if he was putting on the voice. Being honest, Joe wasn't normally the sort of person I would generally hang around with. With time, and the more our paths crossed professionally, we eventually became close friends.

We toured the world together – performing for the British and American troops in Combined Service Entertainment (CSE) shows. Although we were different people, we became good pals. The most important thing about our friendship is the fact that we can make each other laugh!

I've laughed a lot with Joe for the last 30 years; I bet that you have, too.

The other secret to our friendship and why it's been so long-lasting is that we have both been there for each other when we needed it most. There's a bond that comes from sticking together through thick and thin. I know that's always going to be there, and it's a part of my life I'm grateful for.

I had no idea Joe was a writer; that's the thing about him – he constantly surprises. His last two books are corkers, by the way, and you should definitely seek them out.

Before I let you turn the page and enter into Joe's dark world, there's something you need to know…

More than all the fun and more than all the scrapes that life throws at us. Even more than the shared laughs, to quote Sir Michael Caine: "Not a lot of people know this."

It's how dark Joe's mind is.

I trust him with my life. I trust him to make me laugh, and now I trust him to scare the life out of me.

If you like your horror dark and funny – but mostly dark, then this anthology is for you.

He's my mate, but for God's sake, don't be fooled by that squeaky voice!

For the Love of Horror
By Paul Kane

Horror.

What springs to mind when you read that word, especially when we talk about horror fiction? Monsters – the staples like zombies, werewolves, vampires perhaps? – a feeling of dread, repulsion? Being scared? Blood and gore? Tension and suspense?

One of the first things people say to me at family gatherings or parties when they find out I write horror is: "But you're so nice. You're so funny. How can you write all that kind of stuff?" And what I've found, after more than a quarter of a century in this business, is that horror writers tend to be some of the nicest, funniest people you'll ever meet. Maybe it's because we get all the things that frighten us down on the page, maybe it's free therapy or something? It's probably best not to look into it too deeply or it all falls apart.

I've been described by the lovely Muriel Gray as 'what a smile looks like distilled into human form.' Jason Arnopp once called me 'fundamentally a humanoid Cheshire Cat.' Guy Adams at one point even called me in an introduction a 'kinky badger,' but that's another story... And yet, I've had reviews which say my work is 'hopelessly grim' or 'full of unpleasant nastiness,' which, honestly, I take as a compliment.

So, when I found out that the author of this book you hold in your hands, one Mr. Joe Pasquale, wrote horror, I probably wasn't as surprised as most people. Unlike Bradley, I've never had the pleasure of meeting Joe, but I have heard what a nice guy he is; it goes without saying he's funny, because that's how most people know him – in his other career as a top comedian.

He's been making me laugh on the telly for decades, apart from anything else. Yet, at the same time, Joe can deliver a gut-punch worthy of a Koontz or Masterton tale. Read 'No Regrets' and tell me that I'm wrong.

My old mate, Stephen Volk, creator of *Afterlife*, writer of *Gothic* and *The Awakening*, once said 'You cut Paul Kane, the love of horror will come gushing out...' Not that he ever has, you understand, although I'm sure he's felt like doing it a few times. His point was I live and breathe horror, have done ever since I was little. I was reading Jim Herbert before I was out of nappies (not quite, but you get the picture), into Clive Barker and Anne Rice before I hit puberty. I know my onions where the genre is concerned, and let me tell you, Joe is the real deal. He's a man who loves horror just as much as I do!

Yes, you'll find certain familiar tropes in here, the same as you do with most writers' fiction, but it's what Joe does with those that makes his stories unique. The imagination employed. When I first read 'The Umpire Strikes

Back' I was bowled over (sorry, couldn't resist). It's a clash of two very different ideas that nobody's ever thought of putting together before. There's chilling body horror in the likes of 'The After Effects of Love,' dark humour in 'The Underwearwolf' (which could be the spiritual cousin to my own 'Dracula in Love'), homages to the classics, but also thought-provoking commentary on life in general (check out 'Granpire' or 'Annus Horribilis'). It's one of the things that makes this particular genre such a powerful one.

Bad things happening to good people (or should I say expertly-drawn characters?). Good things happening to bad people. It's what makes us tick and draws us back to horror again and again.

But, above all else, you're going to have fun. The kind of kick only us horror fans, those who love horror and always have, get out of reading books like these.

Sit back, strap yourself in, and enjoy the ride, folks!

Paul Kane
Author of *The Hellraiser Films and their Legacy*, *Hellbound Hearts*, and
Sherlock Holmes and the Servants of Hell
Derbyshire February 2023

A Word from the Author

When it comes to horror, whatever fiction is written in that genre, nothing is as horrifying as reality, nothing as terrible as the things we do to each other. History shows that we are a deeply flawed species. And, with each generation, we are doomed to keep on repeating the same patterns until we eventually snuff ourselves out.

Maybe, hopefully, one day, the light might switch on, and the spark of humanity that gives us so much more than we deserve may just help us finally break the cycle of horrors we inflict to not just our own kind, but to anything else living upon this earth – and upon the planet itself.

It is that which gave me the inspiration for these stories.

I first found my way to reading books as a child not through the usual route of Enid Blyton and/or Beatrix Potter, but through an entirely different path. That path led me to Edgar Allen Poe, Bram Stoker, H.P. Lovecraft, and Mary Shelley. Obviously, as an 8-year-old, that may seem a little advanced – so, I started with John Steinbeck's *Of Mice and Men.*

It blew me away.

It still does – because it shows us *real* horror. It shows the best and the worst of us, and it was the first time I had ever experienced real fear while reading a book – even though there is nothing 'horror' in the narrative itself; no, you will never find it in that section of any bookshop. *Of Mice and Men* is a true classic, a work of genius, a study of the human condition. As I read, I felt the tension and anxiety in my belly as I *knew* it was leading me to some massive event that would change everything – even my life!

(Spoiler alert): When George killed Lenny at the end, it broke my heart. I was devastated. I broke down. How could the man Lenny trusted – not just a man, but the only human he trusted – do that to him? I have read *Of Mice and Men* many times since I was a kid, and it gets me every time.

Then came William Golding's *Lord of the Flies*, and that scared the living shit out of me! I'd experienced some bullying at that point in my young life and I didn't like it – not one bit. But *Flies* showed me that even as young children, given the chance, we can be absolute bastards.

I made the gentle transition to H.G Wells' *War of the Worlds*, Robert Louis Stevenson's *Dr. Jekyll and Mr. Hyde*, Poe's *Masque of The Red Death* – it was then I knew I was ready for the big hitters: *Dracula* and *Frankenstein*. I'd seen the old Universal movies, but they didn't scare me at all.

However, books *did.*

It was one small step to Ray Bradbury's *Something Wicked This Way Comes*, and my education had only just begun. It's a lesson that never ends.

We don't really *need* more horror fiction; there's enough real-life horror out there without us inventing others – but we do it because, in some strange way, horror brings us some light relief from those real monsters in our lives.

Sweet dreams.

Joe Pasquale

OF MICE and WOLFMEN

The Umpire Strikes Back

LOCATION: Mortuary in the town of Carlton – 2km from Melbourne, Australia.

TIME: Day 6 of the Test Match, Australia VS England. 1.35 a.m. precisely.

*O*h, fuck me... What's going on?
      I don't know how long I've been here... I just know it's been a while... I can still see clearly, yet I know my eyes are only half open...
When I say I can see, I mean I can make out shades of darkness and light – it all keeps flashing by in a dull, blurry mess above my head, like clouds passing the sun... I think I'm in a room with strip lights and ghosts wandering about...
What the fuck *is wrong with me?*
I'm here, lying on my back without a fucking clue, and I hear the irritating buzzing of the lights as neon gas gets excited in its cigar-like tube and fluoresces. And I can't remember a fucking thing...
I hear the ghosts' voices. Muffled. I can barely make out what they're saying, so I listen harder. It's something about... a tree stump?
I can't move any part of my body. I can't say anything. But I can hear and I can see....
I cry – but I don't shed a tear or make any sound at all.

TIME: 1.40 a.m.

My silent sadness is interrupted by the noise of a thick, heavy zip being undone. The sudden intrusion of light blinds my half-open, still eyes as the ghost opening the zip turns out not to be a ghost after all….

It's a man.

He speaks.

"*Fuuuck…* Oh, Jesus H. Christ on a fucking stick… what the fuck is *this*?" His voice is thick with an Australian accent.

Oh, dear God, I think I'm in a body bag!

I'm naked. I can't move my head to see what's going on, but there's a small magnifying mirror just in my eyeline.

I see two men: one is dressed like a surgeon, the other wears the pale blue scrubs more of a hospital porter. I also see a large piece of bloodstained wood protruding from my chest – it's pale brown and about 2-foot long.

The surgeon opens up the body bag all the way down and steps back to scan me from head to foot.

"Is that a fucking *cricket stump*?" he asks the porter.

The porter nods sagely and pulls out a pack of cigarettes. He taps it on the palm of his hand, and one of the filtered cancer-tubes pokes its head out. He puts it to his lips and sparks up the flint from a Zip lighter he conjured from thin air.

The surgeon looked to me to be some 30 years older – at *least* - than the porter. I put him at probably in his mid-sixties. He has mad professor hair – a lot like Doc Brown in *Back to The Future* – and a wrinkled, saggy neck that reminds me of a turkey's wattle. I can tell the younger man, the porter, is a waster, an air head, just from the way he talks – or *doesn't,* as the case seems to be.

Illiterate wanker

Even dead, I can tell there's nothing going on behind his eyes except for illegal drugs and fucking.

"You can't smoke a cigarette in here," Doc Brown snaps. "It contaminates the body."

"He's fucking *dead,* isn't he?" The porter protests; the name tag on the left breast of his bland scrubs informs me his name is Gonzales "Not like he's gonna get lung cancer, is it?!"

How can I possibly be dead?

I can hear every word of what the two are saying. I can see *them. The acrid stench of bleach in the room is burning my nostrils… how can that happen when I'm not even breathing? My chest isn't going up and down with even the shallowest of breaths, my lungs aren't taking in oxygen and releasing carbon dioxide....*

So... how am I smelling the fucking bleach?

With a smoky snort, Gonzales stubs out the cigarette on the stainless-steel table upon which I'm lying and slots it behind his pierced ear. Then, he reaches into the breast pocket of his tunic and pulls out a tightly rolled doobie.

"What about a touch of the green stuff?" Gonzales says, wafting the white paper cylinder under Doc Brown's nose.

The old surgeon scowls and says, "Look – just let me get this underway. Then we can fire that up. I want a clear head for this because I wanna know what's going on here. Once I've opened the stiff up – maybe then we can kick back and have some fun."

Gonzales tuts and pops the doobie back in the pocket it came from.

TIME: 1.50 a.m.

"So, what happened to this poor bloke?" asks Doc Brown.

"Oh... this is *so* fucked up." Gonzales tells him. "You're not gonna believe this."

"*Really*?" says Doc. "Try me – I'm all ears... hold on, just give me a sec' to get this fucking stump out."

I watch the doc with the wild, white hair snap on a pair of rubber gloves. Then, he grasps the wooden stump sticking out of my chest with both hands....

He pulls.

I feel my back arch and lift off the cold trolley as he tugs.

"Stubborn fucker, ain't ya?" he snarls at the stump. Then he pulls on it again – after getting a tighter purchase.

It doesn't budge.

"D'ya wanna put some gloves on and give me a hand instead of just gawping, ya dopey Muppet?" Doc Brown isn't impressed by the stoner's inaction.

"Yeah, sure." Gonzales sniffs. "But, please, don't call me a Muppet... I fucking *hate* those felt bastards."

The doc keeps on tugging away as Gonzales saunters over to a small cardboard box filled with white latex gloves. Pulling one out, he blows into it and then pulls the inflated mitt over the top of his head. I watch him in the mirror as he does a pretty good chicken dance behind the doc's back.

Doc Brown spins around to slap the porter about the head. "Stop fucking about and help me – or get the fuck out of my mortuary!"

Looking like his feelings are hurt, Gonzales removes the glove from his head and snaps on a fresh pair – on his hands, this time.

"What do you want me to do?" he asks the doc.

"Stand behind him and hold his shoulders down," Doc says. "I'm gonna climb on top –"

Gonzales snorts out a laugh. "You dirty old bugger," he whispers to himself as he rests all his weight onto the top of my arms.

Ignoring the comment, the doctor climbs onto the gurney and sits on me with his scrawny arse just below my rib cage. I can see Gonzales' face level with mine and the look of disgust on it when the pressure of the doc's weight pressed upon my abdomen forces the dead, foetid air out of my lungs in a long, slow rasp which squirts blood from my mouth onto the porter's lips and chin. For good measure, I fart loudly at the same time.

The porter recoils in horror, wiping my dark blood off his face, and the doc laughs his ass off.

"Ha! Serves you fucking right, Brainiac," Doc Brown chuckles. "You might wanna put a mask on. Now, get back on his shoulders."

Gonzales wipes his face with a fist full of wet wipes, which sit in a gayly patterned dispenser on a small table next to mine. He puts on his mask and gets back to holding me down; this time, with his face leaning away from mine.

The doc then puts all his strength into retrieving the cricket stump from my rib cage, his pale old face turning quite red.

I let out another loud fart.

I'm not breathing, but even I can smell its vile odour.

"Was that you or him?" Gonzales giggles as he gags on my fart's foul stink.

"Shut up, Gonzo." The doc snarls.

"Don't call me Gonzo," Gonzales shouts back. "I'm *not* a fucking Muppet! I told you – I fucking hate Muppets!"

"Fair enough," Doc Brown grunts as he finally yanks the stump from my chest. "There you go, ya stubborn bugger." He passes the stump to Gonzales. "Wrap it up in the paper roll over there and put it on the table. I think the police'll wanna look at it later."

Gonzales does as he's asked as the doc fingers the hole in my chest.

"Well, he was one lucky bugger, I'll tell you that much," declares the doc.

"Why's that?" asks Gonzales.

"Missed his heart by about half an inch!" The doc laughs raucously at his own tasteless joke.

Gonzales joins in the laughter, but he clearly doesn't know what he's laughing at.

I feel nothing. I felt no pain when they yanked the stump out of me. Well, I'm dead and pissed off now… does somebody want to explain to me why I'm dead and how this is happening?

TIME: 2 a.m.

The doc picks up a scalpel from the silver side tray and slits the shape of the letter Y into my chest: shoulders to the top of my breastbone, top of my breastbone – avoiding the hole in my chest – down to my belly button.

That done, Doc Brown peels the skin back to reveal my ribcage. He starts picking out fragments of splintered rib bones nestled in the crevasse of my chest with a pair of fine-nosed tweezers.

"So…" the doc grunts. "What's the score here? D'ya know what happened? Who did this to the poor guy?"

"Well," Gonzales says, and I can see he's excited at being able to tell the story.

"The copper that came in the ambulance with the dead guy said –"

"Wait a minute!" The doc interrupts. He picks up a surgical hacksaw. He dons safety glasses and begins sawing into my sternum.

"Fuck!" Gonzales snaps. "D'ya wanna know or not?"

"Yeah, course I do," the doc tells him. "I'm just getting to the good part now."

I feel the teeth of the saw grinding and gnawing away at my bone. It's jarring my whole body and making my vision shaky, especially with half-closed eyes. I see the enjoyment on the doctor's face, beads of sweat running down his brow to be absorbed by the mask covering his face.

"There." The Doc seems pleased with his efforts. "Now, watch this… you're gonna love it." He places the tips of his fingers along the line he's just cut into my chest. Then, he pushes down to widen the gap…

Doc Brown cracks me open like a goose egg to reveal my internal organs.

"Tadaaaaa!" he shouts, displaying my guts to his sidekick with a theatrical flourish like he's just performed an astonishing magic trick.

Gonzales pulls his mask down and mouths *WOW!*

"I think it's time we fired up that special candle of yours," The doc says.

Needing no further encouragement, the porter pulls out the spliff, lights it, and takes a long, hard draw. He holds the smoke in his lungs for a few seconds before coughing and choking for the next minute. *"Whooooa!* This is strong shit," he splutters.

"Fucking amateur," the doc chastises. "Give it here."

Gonzales passes over the joint – he's still coughing and spluttering, his eyes watering.

The doc takes it from the porter's fingers with the tweezers, pulls down his mask, and places the joint gently between his lips. I watch his eyes close as he sucks on it slowly, taking the smoke deep into his lungs. Then, eyes still closed, he smiles gently as the smoke escapes from his lips with no effort. "Wow. This is some *fucking good* gear," the doc says. "What is it?"

"Dunno," Gonzales tells him with a shrug. "I found it in the dead guy's pocket."

The doc has started to sing. Gently, softly, he's singing the opening refrain to *Bohemian Rhapsody*: *"Is this the real life? Is this just fantasy? Caught in a landslide, no escape from reality. Open your eyes, look up to the skies, and see…"* Grabbing my eyelids, the doc pulls them wide open….

I see it in his horrified face as my eyes shock him back into the room and the job in hand.

"Fuck!" the doc exclaims. "Look at them!" He pointed at my face with a trembling finger. "His eyes are *all* black – all pupil and no iris… look … black as the Devil's arse!"

Oh, this is good. I'm loving *this.*

I watch as Doc Brown passes the spliff back to Gonzales.

TIME: 2.16 a.m.

"So, what did the copper say? I'm all ears." The doc picks up the scalpel and begins systematically cutting my organs free from the housing of my cold, dead body. I say cold, but I feel no actual temperature. I don't feel the chill from the air conditioning unit that's buzzing away in the corner, nor any warmth from the doc's breath on my pallid skin.

For his part, Gonzales just keeps on puffing on the joint as he recalls the story of my strange demise. To be honest, *I'm* just as interested in finding out what my story is – at this point, I'm still none the wiser; I simply can't remember a thing.

"Okay…" says Gonzales. "So, apparently, our dead guy here was watching the cricket match this evening – according to the news, it's been rained off all day. So, it's a nighttime Test Match – us versus the Pommies – and we were well in the lead: 102 in front with 6 wickets to go. We were pissing all over the bloody Poms! So, this guy… *this* guy here… this poor fucker here…." Distracted, Gonzales pauses. "What's that?" he asks the doc.

"It's his liver." The doc places my liver gently into a large stainless-steel bowl. "Do keep going."

"Isn't that much bigger than normal?"

"Oh yeah, its massive. Fucking heavy as well. It's full of blood – more than I've seen in a liver before. Just look at it – it's the size of a fucking bagpipe!" The doc picks my liver up out of the bowl with both hands. Squeezing the end of it between his finger and thumb, he chuckles as my thick, black blood squirts over Gonzales' previously spotless tunic.

"Fuck, Doc!" Gonzales squeals, still puffing on his spliff. "This was clean tonight!"

Not bothered one bit, the doc plonks my liver back into the bowl. "Carry on, Gonzales, I'm still listening." He then proceeds to slice out my spleen and kidneys as the porter picks up the story.

"Anyway," Gonzales says. "So, this poor fucker is just sitting there enjoying the cricket, when suddenly the umpire goes fucking mental. He's screaming and shouting some fucking nonsense about evil, the end of days, the Dark Lord – shit like that – and then runs to the centre of the field, grabs one of the stumps, and runs toward the boundary. Then the crazy bastard launches himself into the public stand and stabs this poor fucker right in the chest with the stump. Kills the poor bastard stone dead."

Fuck yes. That's it. It's starting to come back now. I'm beginning to remember….

"So," asks the doc. "Is this guy a pom?"

"Yeah, I think so." Gonzales says.

"Well then, he fucking deserved it!"

They both laugh uproariously at my misfortune.

Fucking Aussies – no class.

TIME: 2.19 a.m.

I watch as the doc once again plucks the spliff from Gonzales' lips and takes a few more tokes on the barge before placing it on the side table.

"What you gonna do now, Doc?" the porter asks.

Doc Brown answers with one, simple word: *"Brain."*

Grinning, the doc pulls the mask back over his mouth and picks up a small circular saw; it reminds me of the kind you'd buy at B&Q, only shinier. Deftly, he cuts around the top of my skull and removes it by twisting slightly as one would a child-proof medicine bottle. As I feel every part of it, I imagine it's like taking the top off a hard-boiled chucky egg.

Once again, I felt nothing but the vibration of blade on bone and smelled stink of burning skull from the friction of the stainless-steel saw.

Most peculiar.

Next, Doc Brown gently removes my brain from its protective housing. He holds it up in front of Gonzales like some gruesome trophy.

I begin to get dizzy: the room spins, my eyes are losing vision. I feel faint
No! Don't black out now!

Thankfully, the dizziness starts to pass after a few seconds as I pull myself together – which isn't easy, considering my spleen, kidneys, and liver were in a bowl and my brain was in Doc Brown's gnarly old hands.

"What do you think?" the doc asks his underling.

Gonzales' mask is still under his chin. "Oh… oh… I think its lovely."

"Then lick it," demands the doc.

"What?"

"I said… fucking *lick it,* you Muppet." So saying, the doc pushes my brain into the porter's face.

With great reluctance, Gonzales touches my cerebral cortex with the tip of his tongue.

"Don't *play* with it!" The doc seems angry. "Fucking *lick* it, or you're next." He picks up his bloodied scalpel and holds it to Gonzales' neck.

Terrified, Gonzales starts licking, which makes even me feel nauseous. They're tiny little flicks of the tongue at first, like a snake sensing its next meal, and then the licks get stronger, harder, until he's lapping at my disembodied brain like a dog licking its own arse. Blood had coagulated within the folds of my brain, and the porter laps up the juices oozing from it.

"That's it… that's it." the doc coos his encouragement. "Good boy… *good boy.*"

In all the excitement of the foulness taking place, I see the doc has accidentally nicked the side of Gonzales' neck with the scalpel's keen blade. Looks like he might have caught the jugular – slightly – and blood oozes from the cut, flowing steadily. It's dribbling down his neck to soak into his scrubs. Every beat of the young man's heart pushes more blood from the tiny wound, and neither of the sick fucks notice.

But *I* did.

Both Doc Brown and his porter friend are now leaning over the gaping hole in my chest and licking my brain right in front of my face, lapping and sucking on its juices in some nasty, perverted frenzy.

Then it happens.

A single drop of Gonzales' blood drips from his neck and into my opened chest. Straight on to my exposed heart…

And then… *then* it all comes thundering back.

I remember who I am.

I remember what *I am!*

My heart begins to beat. I feel the nerve endings of my skin again, the muscles in my arms spring to life, and I feel so immensely *powerful*.

Lifting my hands to the doc and the porter's throats, I tear at the soft flesh of their necks with savage grace; my fingers rip open their arteries with ease to let their blood flow into the cavity of my chest.

Shocked, in agony, Doc Brown drops my brain; it lands in my body cavity. It's quite weird, but at the same time, it's funny to see my brain laying there in the middle of my body.

I know it won't be a problem, not now my strength has returned. Sitting up straight, I pop my brain back into my empty skull and put the top of my head back on. Then, I slip my kidneys back into place, along with my liver, spleen, and any other odds and sods Doc Brown had taken out. I don't bother seeing if they're all in the right place – they will sort themselves out all in good time.

TIME: 2.45 a.m.

I sit there for an age, literally pulling myself together, gathering my thoughts – and then one thought pops into to my mind over all the others....

The doc was right – I was very lucky the crazy umpire missed my heart by a mere half an inch, what with me being a vampire and all.

The Underwearwolf

The trick to life is to not get too attached to it.

Babies are born in blood and chaos, stars and galaxies blast into being amid massive primordial cataclysms, yet a natural human death comes to us like a dog with a broken pelvis dragging its arse behind it and leaving a trail of shit in its wake.

It's not until you witness something like a total eclipse of the Sun that you realise there's a far bigger power than mankind moving those giant chess pieces around the galaxy, turning the universe into God's own celestial clock. You also see nothing is by accident – such as the fact that, by pure coincidence, the Moon is 400 times smaller than the Sun, but also precisely 400 times closer to the Earth than the sun. And that gives our moon the appearance of being the exact same size as the Sun, which allows it to block the star completely and dominate the sky to bring darkness when we should be swathed in the much bigger Sun's light.

Personally, I don't think it *is* pure coincidence.

It just *can't* be.

I'd never witnessed an eclipse before – not until August 1999. Well, when I say *witnessed*, I was working when it happened, and everybody else enjoyed it. I, myself, was somewhat distracted; seriously, though, what could be more important than watching the heavenly bodies that keep us alive dance with each other in the absolute blackness of space?

In my humble opinion, the Moon is just as important as the Sun: it keeps us balanced. For example, without the Moon, there would be no seasons – that lifeless rock keeps us regular, on a timetable, it means we aren't spinning out of control, it moves the oceans and gives us our tides. And, when the Sun is aligned with the Moon – as it was on that particular day a lifetime ago – we get double its gravity, which gives rise to the spring tides.

Now, just imagine what kind of immense power it takes to drag such huge bodies of water from one side of the planet to the other!

No, the Moon definitely isn't something we should underestimate. It brings us other things as well… it brings out the *unknown* in some people.

I didn't underestimate the Moon's power back then, and I never will. After all, it's where the word '*luna*tic' comes from!

Sitting in my office, I had the thick drapes closed as usual; the only light in the room came from the half-dozen or so thick, white church candles I'd scattered around the place.

A client lay on the couch telling me the most intimate secrets of his past and present and his hopes for a future he might or might not live to experience.

I'd learnt over my years as a therapist that, without the free offer of a choice of the best smoke in town or some nice bong cake, it would normally take a new client at least 3 weeks before they were prepared to divulge the kind of stuff he was telling me.

The soft drugs were all quite legal, of course – after all, we were in Amsterdam – and I'd find many clients were quite reticent in taking a puff or a bite of a small cake at first. They'd need loosening up, a little encouragement, so I'd roll up the spliff in front of them to let them see exactly what they were gonna smoke. Then, I'd light it up and take the first toke myself. Once my client was in the moment, we would pass that doobie back and forth and they would talk.

Alternatively, I'd have some cake first – I'd call them *love muffins* – they were always my favourite. There'd be blackberry, raspberry, strawberry, apple – you name it, I had it. I even had Marmite ones for the *real* weirdos!

I had a Lazy Susan in the middle of the low table. Arranged upon it were the various smokes on offer – all in small wooden boxes – along with the full range of love muffins on a silver platter. There'd also be the small sterling silver cake slicer, which had my initials – SVH for Sarah Van Helsing – inscribed in fancy calligraphy on the underside of the blade.

Often, I'd find myself sitting opposite some very strange characters indeed. I just reckoned it went with the job. If you're a psychotherapist, it's gonna happen, and I think with the name *Van Helsing*, I attracted more than my fair share of some real fucking 'head the balls' Hannibal Lecters!

I actually think my name attracted the *truly* disturbed patients; they'd all read *Dracula* and found something compulsively attractive about my name. I believed they hoped they'd come along to sit and chit-chat with a real-life vampire slayer!

How very wrong they were….

However, the patient that one particular day way back in August 1999… there was something quite *different* about him. Well, there were a *lot* of things about him that were *very* different.

He was scared, much like a lot of my clients on their first sitting. He wasn't scared of me, though, or the session, or what he was going to reveal to me....

I kind of got the impression he was scared of what he might *do*.

Most clients begin by talking about the weather for a good 10 minutes while they weighed me up. Or, they'd start questioning me about my background: did I have any mental problems? Who do I go see when *I* don't feel right? That sort of thing. But, right from the off, the guy was different.

He'd come with a purpose…

The old wrought iron, bat-shaped door knocker banged hard against the portcullis-styled door that led into my courtyard. I greeted my new patient with a warm smile through the square holes of the heavy gate. I felt the gothic look went nicely with the image of my ancestral character name in Stoker's famous book.

"Mr. Talbot?" I greeted him. "You're my 10 o'clock."

He simply nodded as I pulled the chain on my left that lifted the gateway.

"Watch your head," I said as he walked forward; he narrowly missed the bottom beam of thick wood.

Mr. Talbot paused and looked back at me in silence as I lowered the gate.

I walked past him. "This way," I said and led him into the small hallway, and then up the iron spiral staircase to my treatment room. It was more of a library, really, something that resembled a Sherlock Holmes-esque study.

"Please… take a seat. Relax, take your shoes off and put your feet up – make yourself comfortable." I gestured to the dark brown leather Chesterfield chaise lounge.

I took my seat at the table in my captain's chair that matched perfectly the antique chaise lounge Mr. Talbot lay upon. "Looks like there's a bit of crowd building up out there." I made light conversation. "All waiting for the big moment?!"

He totally blanked me.

"Would you like a spliff?" I offered. "Or maybe a cake?" I began rolling a joint of the best Moroccan black I had at my disposal.

Mr. Talbot ignored me again.

Then, he closed his eyes and began to talk; he'd not even had a smoke or a cake.

"I tink I'd best start wit my name." He spoke with a thick French accent; I could tell from the twang he was French Canadian – they have a slightly different lilt to the native French people.

"I know your name is Lawrence Talbot," I said. "You told me that on your application form."

He opened his eyes and turned his head to look at me. "So… are you related?"

"Sorry?"

"To 'im?"

"Who?"

"*Abraham* Van Helsing, of course! Are you a descendant? Tat's why I'm 'ere. Tat's why I chose you… no one else can 'elp me…"

I saw he was getting tense: the thick, blue vein in his forehead began to pulse, the muscles in his jawline tightened.

"I'm sorry," I said. "No, he wasn't real. Abraham Van Helsing was a fictional character in a fictional book. It's a great book, I'll give you that, but it's still a work of fantasy."

"Bram Stoker never tought tat. He said it was *all* true, a biography of sorts, and not a ting of entertainment. It says so on ze Internet."

"You want to be careful what you read on the Internet, Mr. Talbot."

"About tat…" my patient said. "It's not my real name. Well, it *was*, but not anymore! I changed it by deed poll, you see."

"So, what do I call you?"

"Asmodeus." He spoke quietly.

Surprised, I sat back in my chair. "King of the Daemons," I said, raising an eyebrow.

"Don't mock me," he snarled.

"I'm not mocking you," I defended. "I'm just surprised you didn't go for Lucifer or Beelzebub."

"I'm not a fucking idiot," Mr. Talbot – *Asmodeus* – snapped. "I wouldn't dare take 'is name in vain."

"I see… If I remember correctly, according to Jewish legend, Asmodeus was in love with the daughter of Raguel… *Sarah*, I think? He killed her seven successive husbands on their wedding night."

"You know your stuff." He smiled.

I lit the spliff I'd rolled earlier and took one long drag; I held it in my lungs for about 30 seconds to let my bloodstream absorb the drug and then let the smoke find its own way out without blowing. Immediately, I felt the lightness take away the furrows in my brow and the tension from my mind.

And then Mr. Talbot hit me with it.

"I'm wearing ladies' underwear!" he declared.

I coughed and laughed at the same time; the smoke in my lungs expelled so fast it burnt my throat and the back of my nasal passage. I began choking.

Mr. Talbot looked disgusted with my reaction. Admittedly, it wasn't very professional of me, but it had come as a bit of a shock – considering he'd just informed me he was King of the Daemons.

"I'm so sorry. I really am," I spluttered. "I just wasn't expecting –"

"It's okay," he said. "I'm just glad I finally told someone."

I took another long, slow drag on the spliff – I needed it.

"I am wearing Victoria's Secret today." Standing up, he smiled, dropped his trousers, and lifted his black t-shirt to reveal a pair of pretty French knickers and bra – both matching with a summer-flower, lacy fabric. Once more, I coughed and snorted the smoke like a newborn dragon.

I apologised once again.

My patient was unusually hirsute – not just his chest, but all the way down his torso and thighs, right down to the bottom of his calves. Seeing all that black hair poking out from such a delicate pair of lace panties was more than my professionalism could take, and my snort turned into a full-blown laugh. I had to throw my head back to try to take in some clean air after coughing my lungs up.

Eventually, I calmed myself down and stubbed out the spliff. Sitting back in my captain's chair, I pulled myself together and asked, "Is that why you're here? Because you're a crossdresser? Do you feel guilty about it? Do you need me to help you with your problem?"

"Fuck no!" Mr. Talbot exclaimed. It's not a problem... I don't feel guilty.... I *love* it!"

"So why drop your trousers to show me? Are you an exhibitionist? Is that it, Mr.... *Asmodeus*?"

"*Fuck* no!" he repeated. He sat up and swung his feet down to the floor. "I showed you because you are a woman. I thought you might appreciate my pretty underwear."

"Well... I do," I admitted. "So why *are* you here on my couch?"

My patient paused for a moment before declaring, "Because I think I'm a fucking *werewolf*!"

I'd heard it all.

Picking up the rest of the reefer, I relit it from the church candle on the edge of my desk. I breathed in deeply.

"So... you're an underwearwolf, are you?"

"I suppose I am." He smiled at me, and I actually thought he was flirting. That was the first time I'd noticed how handsome my patient was. His eyes flicked across my body – I was slightly dishevelled from the raucous round of laughter I'd just emitted; my skirt had ridden up to slightly reveal the top of one stocking and two buttons had come undone on my blouse. I watched Mr. Talbot scrutinise my cleavage and the exposed top of my lacy black bra...

He then gave me a full, beaming smile and raised his eyes to mine to meet my gaze. I figured he expected me to pull myself together, but I didn't. Instead, I ran my finger down the middle of my chest, chasing the tiny bead of sweat that had just run down my cleavage. I then licked my finger and smiled back at him.

Mr. Talbot sat back, clearly unsure of how to respond. I sensed he was slightly intimidated.

"Lie back…" I instructed. His eyes lit up. "Tell me why you think you're a werewolf."

"I don't *tink*… I *am*!" he replied.

"Okay, so tell me."

My patient took a in deep breath and began to talk.

"I was born in Quebec in 1939, August 20th. I'm a Leo – "

"Wait a sec," I interjected. "Are you telling me you're 60 years old?'

"Oui… *yes*… I am."

Wow, I thought, *if he's telling me the truth….* "You're wearing very well – your body is quite amazing!"

And, indeed it was – my supposedly sexagenarian patient didn't look to be any older than 30.

Mr. Talbot smiled; his eyes were still closed as he said, "Zankyou. It is ze benefits of being a lycanthrope."

I took another drag on the spliff.

"As I was saying," he continued, "I'm a Leo, and by ze time I was sthree, my fathser took me 'unting every weekend. But with ze guns – *no*. He said sat would be too easy. We had ze bow and ze arrow and ze fishing rod. We would go camping in ze mountains. I learned a lot from my father, and we would hunt ze deer, ze moose, ze bear, ze mountain cats…. He started me off with ze small mammals like ze squirrel, and ze badger, and ze skunks – I had to work my way up to ze bigger animals. But, when I was only 10 years old, my father died."

Mr. Talbot opened his eyes and looked straight at me.

I offered him the spliff, and he took it. He took 5 or 6 short puffs, held in the smoke, and passed the doobie back. The smoke trailed out of his nostrils as he spoke. "'e was killed by a werewolf."

"Are you saying you killed your own father?"

"No, you stupid woman," Mr Talbot grunted. "I wasn't a werewolf then."

"You're not really a werewolf now, either," I replied with a knowing smile.

"Shut up, woman, and *listen*." He was becoming agitated, so I rolled another spliff and sat back and allowed him to continue.

"We were attacked by a bear. My fathser got in between the bear and myself, and, as my fathser began shouting at ze bear and trying to scare it away with a burning piece of wood, ze bear clawed my fathser in ze face. He shouted at me to run away, and I ran as fast as I could into ze woods. As I ran, I felt the swipe of a claw across my back – the pain burned into my skin, and I zthought it was ze bear zat had clawed me.

"But it wasn't. I managed to climb a tree and watched as, out of nowhere, a creature of ze night attacked ze bear and killed it. My fathser was laying in his own blood – I saw it spilling out onto ze snow. Then ze creature looks up at me and curled back its lips – I saw its teeth and ze bear's blood all over its face. Then I watch as it bit down onto ze back of my fathser's skull and crushed his brain out. I saw by ze light of ze fire zat the creature was half man and half wolf – a *werewolf*, Miss Van Helsing. I saw ze back of its head had been injured by ze bear: Zere was a gash from ze top of its head all ze way down to its neck.

"I screamed and jumped down from ze tree. I picked up ze burning log and slammed it onto ze back of the werewolf's head as it fed on my fathser's brain. Ze fur on ze creature began to sizzle and ze skin began to pop. It stopped feeding on my fathser and ran away.

"I waited, I waited, and waited in ze bloodied snow until ze Mountie police found me 5 days later – I stayed alive by eating ze bear. Obviously, nobody believed my story, and zey say my wound was inflicted by ze bear. But I know ze truth of what 'appened zat night, and Zat was nearly 50 years ago. So, you see, Miss Van Helsing, werewolves *are* real."

I decided to play along with my patient's delusion. I knew that to people like him, such fantasies were all very real indeed.

"Have you killed people when you're a werewolf?"

"I tink so," he replied softly. "It is a big regret of my life zat I might have taken life."

"You don't know?"

"No. When I change, I have no memory of what I do when I am ze wolf. But I know in my heart zat I have killed…."

"How often do you turn into a werewolf?" I asked.

"Obviously, once a month. On ze full moon, you silly woman. I am cursed – I 'ave ze mark of ze devil on my 'ead. Come, feel." Mr. Talbot lunged forward, grabbed my hand, and placed it behind his ear. He then rubbed the tips of my fingers across his scalp.

"See, I 'ave ze 3 sixes. Zat is ze mark of ze devil, and zat is why I changed my name. Zis is who I am. Are you not afraid?" he asked me.

"Of what?"

"Of me, of course. Zere is to be a total eclipse of ze Sun in just few minutes time, and zen I will change. Zen you will see zat I am the wolf, zen you will *see*. Zis is why I am 'ere – you must kill me when I change. You must shoot me, Miss Van Helsing." He pulled out an old Smith and Wesson revolver from the waistband of his pants – how it had not fallen out when he'd shown me his frillies was quite beyond me.

"Look… *see*." Unlocking the gun, he showed me that every one of its six chambers was loaded. "Zey are all silver bullets, of course. It is ze only way."

I took the gun from him and immediately emptied the bullets out of the window. I noticed as I pulled back the curtain that the sky outside was darkening: the Moon had begun to cast its shadow over the life-giving Sun. The crowd cheered their appreciation of the celestial clock in the heavens.

"No!" my patient screamed. He grabbed the cake slicer from the table and thrust it into my hand. "You must do zis for me! Zis is silver – yes?"

I nodded.

"Then you must stab me in ze 'eart when I change."

I put the cake slicer in my desk drawer and locked it.

"Listen to me!" I shouted. "Sit down." I pushed him back onto the couch; he resembled a terrified little boy with tears running down his face as he sobbed silently. He evidently believed what he had told me to be the absolute truth.

"Look at me," I commanded.

Mr. Talbot raised his eyes, still sobbing, lingering for a second or two on the outline of my breasts.

"You are *not* a werewolf." I said sternly. "You will *not* change into anything when the Sun disappears. The marks on your head do not make you the antichrist – they are just a collection of small sebaceous cysts. Your real name is Lawrence Talbot, and you're definitely *not* the King of the Daemons. You were not clawed by a werewolf; it was the bear that swiped you as you ran away from it."

My poor patient's face was in his hands as he cried the tears of a man convinced he was about to turn into a wolf.

"'Ow do you know it was ze bear and not ze wolf?" he asked between sobs.

I stepped over to the window and pulled open the curtains. I stared off into the blackness of the aborted daylight and then at the crowd in the square. They were hushed with reverence at the magnificent spectacle in the darkened sky above them.

Turning to face the crying man-boy, I slipped out of my pencil skirt and undid the remainder of my blouse's buttons. I let it fall from shoulders….

And then I yanked the wig from my head to reveal the ragged scar running down the back of my skull.

"I *know*," I told Mr. Talbot, "I know it was the bear that clawed at you because I was there in the forest with you and your father. You see, Mr. Talbot, Victoria isn't the only one with a secret." And, so saying, I curled back my lips to show him my sharp, fearsome fangs.

At that, Mr. Talbot – *Asmodeus*, for Pete's sake – stopped crying and shat himself.

The After Effects of Love

B ack in 2021, the UK started rolling out the vaccine for COVID-19. Most people hadn't even heard of the word *coronavirus* before the disease ravaged the world, even though it had been right there in front our eyes on bottles of cleaning products such as Dettol: the small print on the back said, *"Kills 99% of all known germs, including coronavirus."*

But just how many of us had ever read that?

Well, not me, for starters.

Of course, there was a lot of scepticism when the first vaccine was introduced: how could they possibly come up with it in such a short space of time?

What were the side effects?

Was it safe?

There was much talk of lethal blood clots as a side effect.

I understand people's fears of *'are we being injected with microchips that send signals back to some mainframe computer to record everything we do and everywhere we go?'* and *'Is this some sort of trojan horse technology where, in years to come, it will release some sort of chemical to make us sterile as a way of controlling population growth?'*

When you consider that, in the past, when a pathogen was linked to a disease, the timeline between its discovery and the introduction of a 'safe vaccine' was quite lengthy – you can see why quizzical eyebrows were raised by some people….

For example, typhoid fever was first discovered in 1881 – the vaccine was developed and released in 1896, some 15 years later.

Meningitis – 1889, its vaccine in 1981. 92 years later.

The list goes on…

Whooping cough – 1907, its vaccine in 1949. 42 years to develop vaccine.
Polio – 1908, its vaccine in 1950. 42 years to develop a vaccine.
Mumps – 1950, its vaccine in 1978. 28 years to develop a vaccine.
Measles – 1952, its vaccine in 1962. 10 years to develop a vaccine.
Hepatitis B – 1964, its vaccine in 1981. 17 years to develop a vaccine.
Ebola – 1976, its vaccine in 2019. 43 years to develop a vaccine.
Then…
Sars, COVID-19 – 2019, its vaccine in 2020. 9 months to develop a vaccine.

So, how long had they actually been working on the vaccine?

Well, I can tell you it was a lot longer than the 9 months we were told.

This, then, is the story of the very first inoculations….

August the 20th, 2010.

The marriage of Catherine Rosalind Piller to Chrystopher Alis took place in Bury St. Edmunds, Suffolk. Cat – as she like to be called – had been seeing Chrys for a few years after they met at a Starbucks. Chrys – spelled the German way with a Y – had been working for a pharmaceutical company on the outskirts of Ipswich as a research chemist for 8 years. Cat worked in the Canteen of the same facility, but they'd never met because Chrys always took a packed lunch. At 1 p.m. each day, he'd pull his fold-up chair out from beneath his work station, sit in the corner of the lab, take his BHS flask out from his backpack, pour decaf coffee into the lid/cup of the Thermos, drink precisely 3 small cups of the hot, sweet coffee, open his Tupperware box, and proceed to eat his tuna and cucumber wrap. He'd follow that with a packet of cheese and onion crisps and a small slice of buttered malt loaf.

Chrys was a creature of habit – calm, studious, and dependable – whereas Cat was the total opposite – wild, impetuous, and wholly unpredictable.

As I said earlier, the two met at a Starbucks in Ipswich one Saturday afternoon. Chrys had been to his weekly squash game with his lab partner, Rob. Fitness was important to Chrys – healthy mind, healthy body, and all that.

Cat couldn't give a shit about any of that nonsense. She'd been out the night before with some of the other girls from the work's canteen and got so pissed she'd not woken up until midday. With no coffee in the house, she'd schlepped round to Starbucks in her dressing gown and slippers for her customary black coffee with an extra shot. Then, she'd slumped into the corner of an L-shaped bench seat and dozed off.

When Chrys called in for his habitual post-squash coffee, he found a cute girl in her dressing gown sitting in his favourite seat. There were plenty of other seats, if course, but Chrys considered that particular one to be his; it was where he *always* sat. He noticed the girl was very pretty, but that wasn't important to him at that moment in time.

"Excuse me," he said tentatively. "Are you planning on sleeping here for long? It's just that this… this is where I normally sit."

Cat opened one eye. "Fuck off!" she snapped. "Can't you see I'm dying here?" She closed her eye again.

It was a new experience for Chrys. It was definitely the first time a girl had told him to *fuck off*. But, rather than be offended, he surprised himself by laughing. It had amused him.

"Did you just tell me to fuck off?" He laughed.

Cat opened the same eye again and smiled at him. She tried to focus by opening her other eye. "I'm *so* sorry," she groaned. "I'm not in a good place today." Pausing, Cat squinted at the guy through her headache. He was a looker alright – no Brad Pitt, more of a Matt Damon. "But I think my day just got better," she continued with a welcoming smile. Cat then patted the padded pleather seat beside her. "There's room for two if you wanna squeeze in!"

"Weeeell?" said Chrys with some hesitation.

Oh, come on," Cat said. "I don't bite. My name's Catherine – you can call me Cat. I don't normally dress like this – well, not *outside*. I just needed a coffee kinda bad."

Chrys shuffled in and sat next to her. "My name is Chrys – with a Y."

"Why?" Cat asked.

"Yeah, that's right" replied Chrys….

And that was it; they were inseparable from that moment on.

Chrys moved in with Cat 3 weeks later; love had truly bitten them both, and hard. They got married, honeymooned in Venice, and they were in so much in love. Cat loosened Chrys up a little, and he gave her more focus; they were both definitely better together. Within months, he'd weaned his new wife off alcohol binges, and she was finally happy and content to be loved by someone she loved in equal measure.

Over the next few years, they worked to travel. Every spare penny they earned they put away and holidayed as much as possible. Weekends away were their favourite: no more than a 2 to 3-hour flight, 1 small suitcase, and they were off. They'd leave Friday early evening and come back late Sunday night all ready for work Monday morning. Paris, Rome, Cannes, Madrid, Brussels, Southern Ireland, Iceland, Switzerland, Germany….

Then, one day, they were both offered an opportunity they couldn't refuse. All employees at the pharmaceutical company were presented with the chance to apply to take part in a new drug trial. The company was only looking for two subjects, which *had* to be couple, both under 30 years old, of good health, no known allergies, teetotalers, nonsmokers, no previous illegal drug use, and no history of psychological problems.

Cat and Chrys fit the bill perfectly.

They were offered a year's salary – each – for just one month of their time, and they'd be given the rest of the year off!

With Chrys on £60k a year and Cat on £30k, it really was a no-brainer.

"Just think about what we can do with ninety big ones!" Chrys was most excited. "Think about all the places we can go with a whole year to ourselves!"

They signed on the dotted line.

They were to be flown to a secret clinic located in the wilds of Scotland. It was completely isolated from the outside world, and they were allowed no phones, no computers, no tv, no radio, no newspapers, no outside influences at all. There were only the most basic rations of food – and a complete embargo on anything from outside the clinic: books, stimulants, coffee, tea. They were completely sugar-free and had no meat or fish – their diet was completely vegan with just water to drink for 28 days.

All Chrys and Cat had was each other and a medical team to watch them 24 hours a day. But they had each other, and that was enough.

The clinic was completely hidden to the outside world: it had been built underground beneath the ruins of an old castle near Loch Ness that dated back to the time of the Stuarts.

Chrys and Cat were allocated one hour's playtime – as the medical staff liked to call it – and were to be transported by lift to the outside world. There, they were permitted to walk around the grounds of the ruins accompanied by a pair of armed guards. The guards never uttered a single word; if Cat and Chrys tried to start a conversation with them, they were met with stony silence.

Nonetheless, the couple were quite content in their isolation. After all, 90 grand buys a *lot* of patience.

As it transpired, Cat and Chrys only got to 'play' for one day.

They were informed everything would be run like a military operation, which suited Chrys just fine – he liked the regimented way of living. Cat wasn't so easy-going, but her husband kept her calm whenever she got a bit tetchy by reminding her of all the money they'd be getting at the end of it all.

The food was exactly the same every day – served at exactly the same time:

7 a.m. – breakfast: porridge and 1 slightly under-ripe banana.

1 p.m. – lunch: steamed vegetables, soya protein fashioned into a fake beef steak, 2 slices of soda bread with vegetable spread, and 1 apple.

7 p.m. – dinner: more soya protein – fashioned and flavoured to look and taste like fish, pulses, green salad, boiled potatoes, and 6 fresh strawberries each.

They had single beds in the same room, which had a myriad of medical equipment scattered strategically around the room. The beds were close enough for Cat and Chrys to hold hands while laying down in them.

They had no control over the lights. They went out at 10:30 p.m. and came back on again at 6.30 a.m. Then it was time to get showered before breakfast.

Day 1.

Cat and Chrys arrived at the facility in the early evening. They were greeted enthusiastically by the medical team as they were escorted by the pair of armed guards from the military helicopter that dropped them off on a nearby landing area.

Shown to their quarters, the couple were left to relax and unpack their personal items, which was just underwear. Everything else was provided: outer clothes, washing essentials, shampoo and conditioner, comb, hairbrush, shaving kit, toothbrush and toothpaste. Nothing was overlooked – it was like a prison with very friendly guards. The two ate their first structured meal and went to bed.

Day 2.

Breakfast, followed by the induction meeting. There, Cat and Chrys were told in the evening of that day – at precisely 10.15 p.m. – they would be injected with the test vaccine for the coronavirus. They would then be monitored for any side-effects during the rest of their time at the facility. They were both aware of the virus: Chrys because of his obvious knowledge of pharma', and Cat because she used Dettol and actually bothered to read the labels on such things.

They were advised to keep any questions to a minimum and they would be shadowed by a member of staff all day and continually monitored by CCTV during the night. Their vitals would also be monitored, and they were instructed to avoid any sexual contact for the duration of their trial. If they felt anything odd health-wise – absolutely *anything* untoward – they were to immediately let a shadowing staff member aware.

Once that meeting was adjourned, the two had lunch and enjoyed their 'playtime' outside – blissfully unaware it would be the only day they would get to enjoy the sun on their current bodies.

10.15 p.m.

The vaccine was administered.

Cat and Chrys lay in their respective beds and held hands as the vaccine serum was injected simultaneously into their arms by the 2 masked lab technicians – neither of whom had smiles in their eyes.

Cat and Chrys smiled at each other as the drug pumped into their veins.

"I love you," Chrys said.

"I love you too," Cat replied, and, with that, their eyes began to close.

As Chrys's peripheral vision began to close in on him, and before passing out, he noticed a third white-coated technician place a plastic wrist band on him.

It said: *Patient 001 CHRYSALIS.*

He didn't see the band on Cat's wrist, which read: *Patient 002 CATERPILLER.*

Day 3.

Chrys and Cat fell into a medically-induced coma. Their vital signs were all stable, and both were fitted with a canula which drip-fed them to keep their bodies hydrated. They also had an IV in their arm to keep their bodies pumped with essential nutrients….

Day 4.

Heartbeats and pulses slowed to 50% of normal for a human being. The doctors began to ask themselves if their subjects were still human. They knew mankind had to adapt, to change, in order to survive the pandemic; our species had to become something else.

Cat and Chrys's bodies had discharged some form of web-like substance. Secreted through their sweat glands, it put a light coating of a white, gossamer substance over their entire bodies. Their body temperatures reached a fever-height of 115 Fahrenheit, which should've killed them both. But no, they were surviving, and not just surviving – they were growing, *changing*. A bizarre metamorphosis was taking place before the very eyes of the doctors and technicians.

Day 5.

The membrane that had appeared so gently had increased in thickness to create a sheen of an almost rainbow-like quality as it solidified over Cat and Chrys's bodies. Their faces could still be seen through the webbing, but the substance had a strange effect on the strip lighting above their heads: it was like observing the two through a prism or through the many lenses of the compound eye of a housefly.

Day 6.

The webbing had thickened considerably in 24 hours. It had taken on the appearance of armadillo skin and separated into countless tiny platelets, which fit perfectly together like a natural mosaic of shiny grey tiles; it resembled a jigsaw puzzle with no corner pieces.

Attempts were made to X-ray the two subjects, but the rays were unable to pass through the thick membrane. It left the scientists in the dark as to what might be happening beneath the calm, solid exterior.

Cat and Chrys's temperature had risen to 120 degrees Fahrenheit – yet still there was a heartbeat… of sorts. Whatever was in there didn't beat like a human's heart – it was more of a constant hum. But, apart from that, everything seemed to be going to plan as far as the facility was concerned.

Day 7.

The pitch of the internal hum heightened to a frequency that resonated with any glass in the vicinity and made it vibrate. Over the course of the day, the hum intensified and shattered the observation glass between the scientists and their subjects. The glass was replaced with plastic sheets. The monitoring continued.

Day 8.

The humming stopped.

It was replaced by intermittent sounds of cracking. Whatever was beneath the hardened carapaces had started to shift and move, which caused the tiny external plates to rub and grind against each other.

Day 9.

The cracking sounds stopped.

The plates solidified. There was no movement, no heartbeat, no humming. There was just a smell – a god-awful reek that filled the whole unit, one so bad that it caused immediate projectile vomiting from everybody inside the facility the second it hit the sensory receptors in their noses. Gas masks were therefore required.

Day 10.

The ghastly smell remained.

The outer shell of both subjects began to crack and flake away, which made way for a new layer of the tiny plates beneath the spent ones. The bodies of the chrysalids were growing, expanding. The pigment of the new miniature plates changed. The old ones had turned dark brown, but the new came through with the pretty hue of a rainbow beetle – white light reflected from them in a multitude of bright colours.

The new shells were soft at first, but after a few hours of oxidation in the air, they turned as hard as a Kevlar bulletproof vest. The scientists attempted to take a sample of the fluid inside the shell with a lumbar-puncture needle made of tungsten steel – but nothing could penetrate the unnatural wall the pupae had created.

Day 11.

The sickening smell dissipated, and was replaced by a sweet-smelling odour not dissimilar to that of pear drops. Gas masks were no longer required.

Day 12.

The outer shells had expanded to almost double their original size. They had also begun moving slightly. A thick, yellow sap-like substance seeped slowly from between the platelets; it hardened almost the second it touched the air, sealing the membrane shut as it did so.

Day 13.

The colour of the shells had begun to change once more. The outer skin had become slightly translucent and allowed some light to pass through the membrane. And that gave some clue as to what might be going on beneath the surface.

The scientists shone their lights into the shells, tapped at them, and watched the viscous fluids inside move around like tributaries feeding into a river.

Day 14.

The sweet smell remained but grew more potent, and the reason for the incredible growth of the shells became apparent. Beneath the partly-transparent plates, the subjects' cells were changing as their DNA re-sequenced itself. Cells underwent rapid mitosis and new structures were being assembled: wings could be seen forming, giant wings that encased the whole inside of the chrysalids to protect the astonishing changes happening to what used to be Chrys and Cat Alis.

Day 15.

The pupae began emitting a hissing sound. It was assumed part of the cycle was coming to an end. The next stage of development and growth was ready to begin.

Day 16.

The hissing continued. The huge wings could be seen more clearly and appeared to be fully formed.

Day 17.

The day of reckoning.

The facility was manned by three teams of doctors and technicians, all working 8-hour shifts. But Day 17 was what they referred to as the 'totality.' So, all the staff were invited to witness the birth of a brand-new sub-species of *Homo sapiens*. It was only fair because, after all, they were all parents of those new lives, all responsible for their conception and development, and it seemed only fitting they should be there for the birth of their progeny.

The air, along with the sweet smell that had turned rancid, was full of excitement, buzzing with anticipation as everyone watched Cat and Chrys writhe and squirm inside the naturally-secreted suits of armour. It was *happening*, and the faculty became hushed as people held their breath; the atmosphere was heavy with hope and sheer joy.

The pupae had been moving for 3 to 4 hours, but then, suddenly, they stopped.

In that moment of stillness, *everything* stopped. The air conditioning fans quit whirring and the lights went out. It took only a few seconds for the emergency generators to kick in, and in that time, everyone felt a surge of panic in the darkness.

As the red emergency lights switched on, the laboratory's doors locked, the Klaxon blared, and the pupae shells exploded to cover all the gathered medical and security teams in a stinking, viscous spray of amniotic fluid and blood. Everyone screamed and tried to dodge the bloody mess – but failed dismally. Not one person escaped the eruption of shit-smelling broth created inside the cauldron of Cat and Chrys's ever-changing cells.

Slowly, the medics and guards began to calm down, although the latter remained on high alert with their weapons drawn. The whole place was soaked in red emergency lighting as the security Klaxon assaulted everybody's ears. It was finally silenced when one of the scientists punched a four-digit code into a keypad near the door.

They all stood in rapt silence and stared at what used to be Chrys and Cat: what they saw were two *things* with wings wrapped tightly around their bodies.

Slowly, surely, the wings unfurled. As they did so, the facility's red light shone through the thin membranes to show the veins and arteries within filling with blood. They were giant, bat-like wings – leathery like old skin and the span of a family car. And, as the blood engorged them, the wings flapped, and the two creatures hovered above the beds upon which they'd metamorphosed.

The doctors and scientists were confused – not by the wings themselves, but by the fact that the bodies of Chrys and Cat were not like those of some giant moth. They had no insect-like thorax, no half-dozen multi-jointed legs, no antennae, no long, protruding proboscis, no vast compound eyes… what they did have, however, were *teeth*…

Sparkling, ivory *fangs* to be precise.

Of course, the brand-new Cat and Chrys were completely naked: their skin was the colour of new-born babies, totally unblemished except for the blood and juices of their afterbirth, which smeared their bodies like a piece of modern abstract art.

And they were hungry. *Very* hungry. After all, they hadn't eaten for 17 days.

Scientists and doctors alike gasped in shock as Cat and Chrys flew straight at the two closest security guards and plunged razor-sharp teeth deep into their necks; hot, nourishing blood erupted into the creatures' mouths like geysers. The guards' heart rates were through the roof and adrenaline made the blood flow rapidly to engorge their veins.

Cat and Chrys drank until they bled the guards dry. They then turned their attention to the trapped medical staff. They drained each one and tossed their bodies aside like old, discarded skin. In 24 hours, they would all change, too – the bloodless corpses cured of COVID-19, reborn stronger, better, and insatiably hungry.

Cat and Chrys became visibly aroused as they fed – more so than they'd ever experienced as mere humans. And so, they fucked. They fucked violently in the dark river of spilled blood that pooled on the cold, marble floor of the place that had been their home for 17 days. And when they came, it was with an intensity driven by the demons they had become….

In that moment, Cat and Chrys knew what they had to do to save the world – they would just have to feed.

Afterword.

So… if I were you, I'd have the jab and not give a fuck about the side effects. Very soon, death from blood clots will be a thing of the past.

Abracadaver

The water torture escape.

He'd done it hundreds of times before, probably more – well into the *thousands*. It was like falling off a log for him, but this time it was different: the blackness that took over was thick, smothering. He opened his eyes, and it was as if the whole world was soaked in sepia... and then the darkness swallowed him completely.

When he eventually opened his eyes again, he was sitting in a train carriage. Blood poured from the walls to pool at his feet; it ran in little rivulets of gore from every corner of the carriage and smeared the windows, which obscured his view of the vile obscenities he just *knew* lurked on the other side. A strange mist began to rise from the bench seat opposite and, as it began to take form – not entirely solid –it fashioned itself into a human shape.

"Where am I?" he asked the shape of mist, even though he knew in his gut he was in Hell.

The face of a demon swirled into focus through the mist, but only for a few seconds. It was still long enough for it to smile at him and say, "This is your train of thought." Then, its features softened into the face of an angel – the face of his *mother*.

"Which are you?" he asked, "angel or demon?"

"That is for you to decide," the mist-shape replied. "But this train of thought is coming to its next stop. Time for you to go." The shape evaporated into the blood-soaked carriage, and once again the darkness took him.

He awoke to the sound of a loud banging ringing in his ears. Opening his eyes, he realised he was back in the water tank, suspended upside down. The stage lights created myriad prisms through the water and rainbows that danced before his eyes. He gasped for air as his lungs filled with water, and he felt his brain swelling inside his skull as his cerebral cortex struggled to function through being starved of oxygen.

Through the rainbows, he saw the banging was coming from the axe his assistant was using to try smashing the glass coffin to release him from the icy grasp of death.

One more *thwack* and *clang* of the axe, and the release of pressure in his head came with the shattering of glass. Then he was on the floor like a beached whale gasping for breath. He was unaware of the screams from his audience; he bled profusely from his nose, eyes, and ears.

Two stage assistants lifted him to his feet and raised both his arms to the audience, who all cheered their approval.

All except for *her*.

She was Victoria Polidori. She was a psychic of sorts – not so much a mind reader – her specialty was more that of being a *messenger*. Harry Houdini had planned on visiting her very soon because she was on his list of mediums to discredit. He'd made it his mission in life to expose charlatan clairvoyants because he fully believed *no one* had the power he sought.

After the death of his mother in 1913, Houdini became obsessed with contacting her on the 'other side.' He began visiting as many 'psychics' as he could – it was a trend that had hit its halcyon days in America and Europe in the early part of that century, and they were literally *everywhere*. After each session, Houdini was angered by the fact they were simply frauds preying on the vulnerability of people in the saddest days of their lives. Often, such 'psychics' would use the same stage tricks he and his wife, Bess, had mastered in their early days as travelling troubadour magicians: misdirection and sleight of hand. It was all very basic stuff for a magician of Houdini's pedigree, but to the layman looking for contact with loved ones from beyond the grave, they were very convincing indeed.

Houdini said there were only 5 types of illusion:
1. Appearance.
2 Disappearance.
3. Penetration.
4. Levitation.
5. Transformation.

Every trick was derived from one of those types of illusions – and the 'psychics' would use every single one of them in their fake seances.

Houdini spent the last 20 years of his life debunking the fraudsters, yet all the while seeking that one real spark of hope – a true psychic who could contact his dead mother.

He was great friends with Sir Arthur Conan Doyle for many years. Conan Doyle was a true believer in things of an occult nature, and even believed

Houdini himself had powers gifted from the dark side. That was, until one day in 1922, Doyle's wife held a seance for Houdini with the sole purpose of getting him in touch with his mother's spirit.

The séance was held in the Ambassador hotel in Atlantic city, and Lady Doyle tried to convince Houdini contact *had* been made with his mother, Cecilia, by producing automatic writing…

Houdini lost his temper and declared the evening a sham, a farce, and accused Lady Doyle of being a fraudster as his mother could not speak, read, or *write* English when she was alive. After that, Harry Houdini and Arthur Conan Doyle became the worst of enemies.

Throughout the years, Houdini continued to call out the fakes and charlatans, and as his fame grew as a medium-buster, he took to dressing in elaborate disguises and inviting along journalists and undercover policemen to the meetings. As a result, many famous 'mediums' of the day were exposed – such as Joaquin Argamasilla, known as the 'Spaniard with X-Ray Eyes,' who claimed he could read handwriting or numbers on dice through lead-lined boxes. Houdini very quickly exposed the man as a fraud and a cheat.

Houdini offered a substantial cash prize to anyone who could prove the existence of contact with the other side. The money was never collected.

He'd also exposed many of Victoria Polidori's peers. Most of them were cheap, dog-arse, dirty fleecers, who used all the old tricks unwary punters would easily buy into. To Madame Polidori, however, some were not as fraudulent as Houdini claimed. She genuinely felt that, although they might not have *real* powers, they were offering great comfort to people who needed it at their lowest moments and giving hope that, one day, they'd be reunited with their loved ones.

One such individual was Victoria's mother, Zena Lupei, who was born in Romania in 1872. She travelled the lands as a clairvoyant with a bunch of troubadours, and eventually found her way to America in the late 1890's. There, she set up on her own as a spiritualist in the upper Midwest and travelled around the Great Lakes to bring comfort to the grieving. She had her daughter, Victoria, in tow – it was just the two of them because Victoria's father died just two weeks before she was born on August the 20th 1908.

He was tragically struck by lightning.

Victoria was brought up in a travelling caravan by her mother, who constantly claimed her father was talking to her on a daily basis. He became an imaginary friend Victoria would talk to on a daily basis while her mother didn't realise her daughter was *really* communicating with her dead father. Victoria and her father would laugh secretly to one another about the lies Zena would tell her daughter about what he'd supposedly said to her from beyond death – blissfully unaware of her daughter's power.

Zena was harmless though: She'd use none of the elaborate cons the high-end 'clairvoyants' practiced in their 3-story town houses: no ringing bells, just pure, cold reading, at which she was incredibly good. Not just good, though, Zena was the *best*. Using nothing but tarot cards and a crystal ball, she could draw the life story from a dead cat! If she felt confident, she'd try some channelling – during which she'd profess to be possessed by the grieving person's dead relative or friend who had passed over. Occasionally, Zena would bring Victoria in to 'act' and add a touch more pathos into the scenario.

That was until Harry Houdini paid her a visit.

He wasn't particularly looking for her – it was literally just a chance meeting. Houdini was on his way back to New York after a week's engagement in Minneapolis when he stumbled upon Zena and Victoria's trailer purely by accident. He reckoned she would make another quick and easy notch on his belt of debunked so-called psychics. So, he donned the fake moustache and wig he always carried with him – not that he needed them, as Zena had no idea who he was. To her, he was just another punter looking for some comfort in their search for a meaning to existence.

Victoria was always kept out of sight in the back of the caravan and told to keep quiet until she heard her cue, which came when Zena rapped her knuckles 3 times upon the table. Then, Victoria would pull a thin cable that would slowly douse the candles strategically placed around the caravan by releasing small amounts of water onto the wick and thus extinguishing the flame. Victoria would then emerge slowly from behind her mother dressed in a pinafore dress, her eyes blackened with soot to appear sunken. Her little face would be whitened with makeup, her lips pale and bloodless. A small curtain would open and, balancing on a spring platform behind Zena, Victoria moved up and down. That would create a crude floating effect – almost – that convinced no one but the most gullible. The effect was enhanced by her being lit by a small oil lamp to give an ethereal glow from behind.

Victoria would then launch into her script of talking in tongues, at which point her mother would declare herself an emissary from the other side and interpret what the ghostly young girl was saying. Using the knowledge she'd gleaned from the punter prior to the séance, Zena would tell them what they wanted to hear and send them on their way happy in the knowledge they'd made contact with the other side and received a message from their loved one.

To Victoria, it was all just a game, a game she loved as a small child – up until that fateful day.

Houdini climbed the 4 wooden steps up to the trailer and saw the top half of the small stable door was open. Inside, he saw Zena sitting among her regalia of beads and sashes and other psychic paraphernalia – the caravan was adorned with all manner of talismans and crystals, shrunken heads, and an odd rabbit's foot or three.

He tapped on the open door and Zena waved him in. Houdini pulled the bottom part of the stable door open and stepped inside. Zena quietly shushed an unseen accomplice. She then gestured to her guest to sit down.

Why am I here? he thought to himself, *this is far too easy*, and actually decided to leave the woman alone. He sat for no longer than a second or two before standing up again.

"Please stay," said Zena. "I can help you."

Houdini stood there and held the woman's gaze for more than just a moment while she scanned him inquisitively. He knew she'd be searching him for any clues he might give away, which she could use during her 'reading,' but he knew he was a closed book to her.

And so it began.

Zena started to peck away at him, digging for any glimpses of what or who he had lost. The more she pushed, the less he gave away. She dealt out the tarot cards, all the while asking him leading questions until, in the end, Houdini gave her what she was looking for. He knew he couldn't declare her a fake unless she properly exposed herself.

"I'm trying to make contact with my mother," he told her.

Zena smiled. She was in, and he had her right where he wanted her….

Three knuckle raps on the table. The candles went out. Zena began her labored breathing and eye rolling. The curtain opened and the little girl made her appearance, her head moving slowly side to side as if she was lost and looking for something.

Or *someone*.

Victoria then focused on Houdini. Staring deep into his eyes, the girl began to sob and he felt *something* – and his eyes were forever burned into hers.

As the little girl began to speak in a language he'd never heard before, Houdini was offended. *This isn't even a language*, he thought to himself.

Standing up abruptly, Houdini screamed, "You, Madam, are a *disgrace*!" He pulled violently at the tasseled table cloth, sending the tarot cards high into the air. The crystal ball smashed against the wall – taking with it the shelf adorned with myriad lucky charms – and the little girl fell backwards into the small, secret room behind her.

Houdini turned on his heels and stormed away shouting that Zena wasn't worth a *spit* of his time as he strode back down the small stairs. He ripped off the false wig and moustache and threw them to the ground. Looking back over his shoulder, he saw the girl at the top of the steps glaring at him – he wouldn't see her for another 12 years.

Had he turned back or waited just a moment longer before leaving, Houdini would've noticed the back of the caravan had caught fire from the oil lamp he'd accidentally knocked over. He'd also have seen the little girl dragging her lifeless mother down the steps, her head smoking from the smoldering scarves she had draped over her face.

But no, Harry Houdini didn't turn back.

Zena's face was blackened and scarred, and Victoria cared for her the best she could. And, all the while, her mother would repeat made-up messages from her dead husband to keep her spirits up.

Zena could no longer work as a 'clairvoyant.' The caravan was a charred remnant of what it was and eventually fell into disrepair; the only thing that survived was the old rocking chair. Since they had nowhere to live, Zena joined a freak show as a mer-monster – for which she wore a makeshift mermaid's tail made from old buffalo hides sewn together. She spent most of the day and night sitting in a glass tank filled with water. She also began to drink heavily.

Victoria was taken in by the freak show owner as an act of kindness. He'd witnessed her speaking in tongues to her mother as she sat by the tank with one hand pressed against the glass just to be close. She was eventually given a caravan of her own to perform as *Madame Polidori the Psychic Beauty*. Victoria was paid 10% of what she took but only gave the show's owner 20% of what she made.

Zena drowned one night in the mer-monster pool. She took her own life after someone held a mirror up while she was in the tank. She was no longer able to cope with the true monster she had become.

Victoria sat at the back of the stalls in the Princess Theatre in Montreal and watched one of the last shows the great Harry Houdini would ever perform. She knew it was the night she *had* to witness because her father had told her to be there….

Houdini died two days later of peritonitis after receiving punches to his abdomen from a student earlier that night in his dressing room. Houdini had always boasted he could withstand the punch of any man. That was, until the over-enthusiastic young man took him unawares and jabbed him hard below the ribs numerous times when he was unprepared. Houdini's pancreas ruptured but still he insisted on doing his water torture act despite the blinding agony.

Before Houdini passed away, he made a pact with his wife, Bess, that if he discovered there was an afterlife, he would find a way to contact her. She would know it was him by using a secret message only she would know – the phrase 'Roseabelle, believe.' Roseabelle was the name of Bess's favourite song – one she sang in her vaudeville act long before she met Houdini. He vowed to search out a *true* medium, someone with real powers, so he could relay to his beloved Bess the truth of the other side.

For ten years, Bess held a seance on All Hallows Eve in the presence of a different medium each year. She hoped one of them would pass along the secret message. None of them did, of course, because they were all fakes. And, after a decade of trying unsuccessfully to communicate with Houdini, on the 31st of October 1937, Bess blew out the candle she'd kept permanently alight beside her husband's photograph and declared to the various clairvoyants present, "Ten years is long enough to wait for any man."

That same night, Madame Polidori lit a candle for her mother and rocked herself to sleep in the old rocking chair while her father sang to her. He sang 'Roseabelle,' and she felt her mother's hand slip into hers.

Granpire

"How old are you now, Granny?" asked S'mantha.

"You should never ask a lady how old she is," retorted the old woman.

"Yes," said S'mantha, "but you're not a *real* lady, are you, Granny? You're a *vampire*."

The old lady stopped washing the dregs of blood from the drinking glasses, turned away from the sink, and replied rather sternly, "Listen, young lady – vampires can still be ladies, you know. And, excuse me for saying…" she put her hands on her hips and pointed at the little girl. "Pot…" She then turned the finger to herself. "*Kettle*. You're a vampire, too, and you're a little lady."

"Yes, Granny, I know. But I'll always be seven years old, won't I? So, I'll *never* be a proper lady!"

"Listen to me, baby," said the old woman. "You, my darling, *are* a lady. You are the most beautiful little lady who ever walked this earth, and nothing will ever change that. You will be beautiful forever, you will never get old, your bones will never hurt, your hair will never turn white. It will always be the same beautiful golden colour it is now, and your skin will always be as soft as it is today."

"But not if I go out in the Sun, Granny. Isn't that right?"

The old woman sighed sadly. "Yes, my darling, that's right."

"I don't remember what it was like being in the sunlight anymore. It was *so* long ago. How old am I now, Granny?"

"Not as old as me, baby, not as old as me."

"Yes, but *how old*, Granny?" insisted the girl. *"How old am I?!"* she shouted.

"I've told you a million times before," the old woman handed the little girl her favourite Mickey Mouse mug. "Now, drink up your blood like a good girl – you're looking a little pale tonight."

The little girl gripped the mug by Mickey's ears, which doubled as handles, lifted the mug to her lips, and sipped at the blood.

"Urgh! It's cold!"

"Well, that's not my fault, is it now?" the old woman scolded. "It was warm when I poured it half an hour ago."

"Stop moaning at the girl," said the old man sitting in the wicker chair in the corner of the kitchen. "Here, baby, have some of the fresh stuff." Deftly, he opened up the artery in his wrist with his fangs and waved the little girl over.

Mug in hand, the girl ran to the old man. She lifted the top of Mickey's head off and giggled as the old man filled the mug to the brim with his warm, dark blood. "Stir it up, baby – it'll go down easier."

She sipped the blood through Mickey's nose and smiled as the warmth of the old man's plasma hit her stomach. It never ceased to amaze her how his blood could be warm when his body was as cold as the grave he'd risen from.

"Mmm… that's *much* better, Granpa. You have the best blood I *ever* tasted!" Tilting the mug higher and higher, the little girl chugged the old man's blood, draining the dregs until it was all but gone. Then she lifted Mickey's head off again and licked out the remaining blood with her long, lithe tongue. Done, S'mantha lowered the mug, leaving her chin and nose smeared with little red clots.

The old man laughed. "You look like the cat that got the cream. C'mere, you little rascal." He pulled out a white handkerchief from his waistcoat pocket and spat on a corner of the white cloth. He then dabbed away at the girl's blood-stained little face.

"Well, *that's* not very hygienic, is it?" scolded the old lady.

"Give it a bloody rest, woman!" the old man snapped. He held his thin emaciated arms out, and the girl jumped gleefully into his lap. They cuddled, and it was a cuddle filled with the love one can only feel from a grandad. It was a cold hug, physically, cold from the lack of body heat between the two, but nonetheless, it was still full of love.

The girl pulled at the old man's watch chain and a pocket watch fell from where his hanky was stored. It was a solid gold, 17-jewelled Hunter, and quite priceless. The girl played with the watch a few seconds before inadvertently pushing the top button. The case popped open to reveal the timepiece's ornate face and, on the inside of the case opposite sat a faded picture of a woman. It was cracked and faint with age – but her face was still discernible.

"Granpa? Who's that lady?" asked S'mantha.

The old man and old lady locked eyes for a moment. The old lady shook her head slowly. "No… *don't*," she whispered. "She's heard it enough times."

"Yes, but I like telling it." replied the old man.

The old lady's eyes filled with tears. She held them back. "Okay. If you must" she said. She pulled up a chair and sat her tiny, skinny frame down opposite the old man and the little girl.

The old man lifted S'mantha's face so she would look at him. She kept pulling away, though, mesmerised by the old watch. "Listen, baby," he said as he lifted her face once more, "do you want me to tell you about the lady in the watch?"

"Yes, yes, *yes*!" said the girl excitedly.

The old man looked to his wife, and she nodded slowly. He then once more looked at his granddaughter.

"Baby…" he said quietly. "You are 157 years old!"

"Whaaaat?" laughed the little girl. "I must be older than you, Granny!"

The old lady smiled softly.

"Stop your joshing, Granpa," the girl said. "Tell me about the lady in the watch."

"Baby," the old man began. "I'm 211 years old, and your grandma here is 209 years old. And that lady in the watch – she was your mummy. You were only a tiny baby when she died."

"Wow," gasped the little girl. "What was she like, Granpa? Was she *really* pretty?"

"Oh, yes," said the old man. "She was as pretty as you. In fact, you look just like her, you know."

Smiling, the girl looked at her Grandparents. "I know you've told me before, but tell me again, Granpa. What happened to my mommy? I can never remember. Sometimes, when I'm asleep, I have daymares – and they scare me."

"Don't worry," said her grandfather. "They're not real. They're just bad dreams."

"Yes... but sometimes I hear the noises outside of my head, and it doesn't seem like a dream. I hear the crying – and then it stops. That scares me."

Even though she'd been on the earth for 157 years, S'mantha had no long-term memory. Her mind had reverted back to the child she once was; her body had remained that of the child she'd been when she'd become undead – a symptom of who she really was. She'd developed Alzheimer's in her 120th year – a sadly common ailment amongst long-lived vampires – and her brain simply couldn't retain parts of her own history. So, her Grandparents told her a fairy story version of what had happened to her mother, and they'd told it hundreds of times over the years.

"Well," said the old man. He took in a huge, weary breath, knowing it was not going to be the last time he would tell the girl the story. "Before you were born, your mummy was in hospital while you were in her tummy."

"Her *tummy*, Granpa? how did I get there?"

"Oh, well…" the old man clearly didn't wish to explain the facts of life to his young granddaughter yet again. "You may remember that your mummy worked for a very rich man."

"What work did she do for him?"

He thought for a second and scratched his temple. He then looked to his wife to help him out.

"She did all sorts of things for him," the old woman added.

"Like *what*?" the girl pushed inquisitively.

"Like washing, cooking, and cleaning. She was just a general dogsbody, really."

"WHAAAT?! She had a dog's body? Could she lick her own bum?" The little girl laughed hard, as did her Grandparents. She stopped abruptly, her smile disappearing in a heartbeat.

"What was the rich man's name, Granpa?"

"It was Alucard, baby," the old man told his granddaughter for what felt like the millionth time. *Mr*. Alucard. He helped your mummy make you."

"*How* did he make me, Granpa?"

"Your mummy and Mr. Alucard made you from love mixed with the tip of a unicorn's horn, stirred with the breath of a fairy, the kiss of a butterfly, and a feather from the wings of an angel."

"Wow" the girl said approvingly. "Was Mr. Alucard my daddy? What happened to him? Tell me, Granpa, tell me, *pleeeese*?"

"He fell in love with your mummy and they got married. When they did, he made your mummy a *princess*."

"Am I a princess, too?"

"Yes baby, of course you are," said Granpa. "You're *our* princess."

"But am I a *real* princess?" S'mantha insisted.

"Yes, you are," the old woman said as she stroked her granddaughter's face with the back of her hand. Absently, she tucked some loose strands of the girl's hair behind her ear.

"What happened to my mummy and daddy?" S'mantha alternated glances between her grandparents' eyes as she searched for the familiar answer to maybe give her the chance of a beautiful memory she could keep hold of.

All the old folks came up with were more lies.

"After you were born, your mummy and daddy had to leave to save all the angels. They were so tired that they had to sleep for a hundred years because it took so much energy to fill you with life. That was your mummy and daddy's job – to save the angels."

"Will they come back and save me one day, Granpa?" The girl cocked her head to one side; she looked the picture of innocence.

"One day, baby," said Granpa. "One day." He sighed again, sad in the knowledge they would be having the same conversation again in a few days. "I think it's time for your bed now, little miss, don't you? It's nearly daytime."

"Just 10 more minutes?" S'mantha clasped her tiny hands together and looked like one of the angels she'd just been hearing about.

She was far from that, but how could her grandparents tell her the truth? How could they possibly tell her she was the child of the vampire king and had eaten her own mother from the inside out? How could they tell her that for 9 months from the day of her conception, she literally chewed her way out of her mother's womb and gorged on her organs? How could they begin to explain that all she'd left behind of her own mother was a mutilated corpse drained of blood and innards and she'd slept the sleep of the dead curled up in the gaping chasm of her mother's ribcage amongst the ruined gore? How could they ever say that her father looked on with nothing but joy and pride as his daughter feasted upon his bride, and laughed as she did so? How could they tell their little S'mantha she was the very first natural vampire, that she was *born* that way instead of being created by the bite of another?

How could they tell her she was responsible for turning her own grandparents into blood-sucking addicts? They certainly couldn't tell her they'd given themselves freely to be her guardians for eternity. How could they tell her that, once vampirism had spread through the entire British Isles, the rest of the world had quarantined themselves from the land of the night stalkers – cutting the once-prosperous country off forever? Every border had been permanently shut, and anyone who tried to leave was immediately executed at the behest of the World Government that had arisen amidst the crisis. It had its own security force sanctioned to kill all and any vampires that attempted escape from England – their special forces were armed with giant ultra violet cannons, which had ensured not one single vampire had got out in over a hundred years.

And how could grandparents tell a little girl that she, and she alone, was the saviour of the human race? They were technically no longer human – and she was the catalyst for their metamorphosis.

The only things that survived the nuclear war were the vampires. When the internal squabbles of the World Government escalated into thermo-nuclear war, and they wiped themselves from the face of the earth, it was vampirism that saved what remained of the species.

How could they possibly tell S'mantha her father was, in fact, Count Dracula, and in her moment of coming of age, she would eventually feast upon him. That was the only way for her to become the true queen she was destined to be. It wouldn't be for another 200 years or so – give or take the odd decade or two – so, no, they wouldn't tell her any of those things.

Even if they did, poor little S'mantha wouldn't remember any of it.

Instead, Granpa said, "No, baby, you can't stay up any longer. You know what will happen if you're still awake when the Sun comes up."

"Yes, Granpa. I get dead."

Granpa scooped the little girl up into his arms. As he walked past his wife, she kissed her two fingers, pressed them against the child's head, and smiled kindly at her.

The old man carried his granddaughter carefully downstairs into the cellar and laid her into the small coffin there. He kissed her tiny hand and said, "Good morning, baby. See you in the nighttime."

Then, Granpa turned to face Mr. Alucard who sat upon his ornate wooden throne drinking his own blood from a thin rubber tube inserted into his neck. He was thin, white, gaunt, the shadow of the magnificent vampire he once was, and yet still he watched protectively over his daughter; he'd kept vigil for 157 years, weak from feasting on himself.

The old man bowed in reverence to the king of the vampires and left the cellar tired and hungry – he knew it wouldn't be long before they would turn on each other. With no food sources remaining after the war, the only things living – but not alive – were their own kind. Cannibalism was all they had left.

He knew that *she* would survive, the child, because she was the daughter of the king. As the only *true* vampire, she would live forever and reign over nothing but herself.

The old man laid next to his wife in their coffin and listened to the fearsome screams only a vampire could make.

It had begun, and all they could do was wait for the sunrise.

No Regrets

T his was his last day: day 27.

He sat naked on the rattan chair, ankles and wrists weeping pus and blood from the cable ties securing him to the wicker seat. One arm was free, and there was a cut-throat razor in his trembling hand.

Shaking, he brought the blade up to his eyes and made ready to slice the cold, sharp steel into his lids....

Pausing there, he cast his mind back to a happier time, a time before all this happened.

Valjean was born August 20th 1961 in the French coastal town of La Touqet. He was one of twins who were far from identical. His brother, Marius, lacked everything Valjean was blessed with at birth. Valjean was beautiful, brown-eyed, a healthy 10 pounds, and even sported a shock of black hair that belied his infancy – straight from the womb, he was physically perfect in every way.

Marius, his twin brother, was barely alive when he slithered out from between their mother's legs. He weighed in at just over 3 pounds and was tragically disfigured: he had a cleft palate, club foot, and all his fingers and toes were joined with thick webbing between each digit.

Their mother died in childbirth. The boys' father blamed the poor, disfigured Marius and damned him to Hell that very night. Not once did he call Marius by his birth name to his face, and he flatly refused to accept him as a child of his own. Instead, Marius' father, Gaston Le Noir, would call him *la diable enfant* – the devil child – and feed him the way one would feed a hamster. He strapped a bottle filled with milk to the infant's cot and used the severed finger from a rubber glove as a teat. In the hope the child might die, Gaston left Marius alone in the crib to find his own way to that awful bottle.

Poor Maruis never once received the love and affection that was lavished upon his brother.

Gaston was a huge fan of French literature. He loved the classics: *The Three Musketeers* and *The Count of Monte Cristo* by Alexander Dumas, *Candide* by Voltaire – but, by far, his favourite was Victor Hugo's masterpiece, *Les Miserables*. For a living, Gaston ran a small, incredibly successful seaside restaurant on La Toquet's seafront.

As the boys grew older, Marius was never seen by anyone. Gaston kept him locked up in his room during daylight hours and only allowed him out to do the menial tasks of cleaning and washing. Marius' room was the old wine cellar, which contained only the basics: a bed with a small pillow and blanket, a small toilet, a sink with cold running water, a bedside lamp with no shade, an ancient black-and-white TV, and a collection of classic recipe books from a bygone age.

From a very young age, Marius taught himself to read from the kids' shows he'd watch every day. To compensate for what had been taken away from his body, he gained a great intellect. Marius educated himself from everything he saw on that old television, but he developed no concept of *acting* – to him, everything he saw on that flickering screen was *real*. Nothing was a soap opera, just a movie, or some dramatic series. Everything Marius saw was a documentary to him.

For Valjean, things were totally different.

He lived the life of a normal, happy boy; he was savvy, for sure, but he wasn't *clever* like Marius. His room had all the trappings of luxury any young person could want, but most of all, he had *freedom*. Forever the golden boy, Valjean's father made him front and centre of his entire world. He was the son Gaston had always wanted: talented and blessed with the voice of an angel. Even when his son was a very young boy, Gaston would get Valjean to serenade the restaurant's patrons with delightful renditions of songs by Alain Delon, Edith Piaf, and Charles Aznavour. It was good for business and a delight for Gaston.

From the old wine cellar, Marius would hear his brother singing above and attempt to join in. Sadly, due to the soft, unformed roof of his mouth, the sound he created was more akin to that of a blue whale. The echoes of his mournful, hollow noises would permeate up through the floorboards into the restaurant above long after Valjean had finished a song. The diners were at a loss as to what the sound could possibly be, and Gaston would joke that the cellar was haunted – much to the joy of his customers, who were fascinated by their evening's entertainment.

Marius never celebrated his and Valjean's birthday. He actually didn't even know what a birthday was until he was 10 and his father threw a mangey old dog down into the cellar, snarled *happy birthday*, and slammed the door shut behind him.

The dog was a sandy brown mongrel with cleft palate; he loved Marius immediately, and Marius *loved* him back and named him 'Dog.' The poor animal couldn't bark properly. Similar to Marius' affliction, its deformity obscured the sounds it could make – any attempt to bark would come out like the honk of an angry goose.

Gaston's restaurant specialised in rarities of French cuisine, which meant he often had dealings with all manner of shady characters for the best tidbits: rare champagnes, truffles, illegal caviars from almost-extinct fish, blowfish, etc. However unpleasant such dealings were, it enabled Gaston to charge the highest prices and attract the rarest of customers; esteemed gastronomes from all over the world came to sample Gaston's delicacies, and his fame spanned the globe.

Gaston Le Noir died at the tender age of 46, leaving his twin sons all alone at just 17 years old.

He had been an incurable insomniac, obsessed with creating more and more spectacular dishes. Gaston would toss and turn all night long, his brain never pausing for one second. Most nights, Valjean and Marius would hear their father's bedside lamp flick on, followed by the sound of him scribbling ideas into his notebook beside the bed. Then the light would click off, but only for a short while until he repeated the process.

All night, *every* night.

The irony of being the only insomniac to die in his sleep would have been wasted on Gaston: he simply wouldn't have seen the humour in that at all.

Following Gaston's untimely demise, the restaurant was passed onto the two young boys.

Valjean continued his father's tradition of keeping Marius – the devil child – in the old wine cellar, and, over the next few years, his voice matured and he became a successful recording artist. He scored number 1 hits all over the world, made countless TV appearances, and went on long, live tours.

While Valjean was away, Marius and Dog allowed themselves the luxury of living in the main house behind the restaurant. There, Marius would experiment with the dark recipes he'd grown up with by using the ancient techniques he'd read about in the old cook books. He'd become a connoisseur of red wines after tasting practically every type in his late father's extensive collection and learning what worked best for which dish through the many tomes at his disposal. Sometimes, Marius would venture out in the dead of night with Dog. To avoid people, they'd crawl through the grate that fed into a rain sewer and led to the sea. There, he would just lay on the beach looking up at the stars. Scared of everything that moved out there in the world, Marius loved the sky.

Valjean made a mountain of money from show business and was a millionaire by the time he was 30. That enabled him to expand the restaurant business – making it bigger, better, more exclusive. He also turned the restaurant into an impenetrable fortress; no one got in or out without Valjean's say so. Not that Marius saw anything of the good life – he and Dog were still kept in that dark cellar, never to be seen.

Valjean understood the *real* money wasn't to be made in show business – it was to be found instead in the greed of the fat cats. And so, he continued his father's obsession with finding the most expensive and rarest of dishes and became the highest authority on foie gras – the engorged liver of a goose or duck fattened by the cruel method of force feeding called *gavage*. The bird is fed a concoction of a grain mash mixed with fats and proteins administered through a tube inserted through its nasal passage directly into its stomach 3 or 4 times a day for a number of weeks. As a consequence, the liver swells to over 20 times its normal size. The bird is then slaughtered and the liver harvested to be prepared as a pate for the palate of the wealthy guests.

Taking the method to even higher stages, Valjean introduced edible gold leaf to the mix: when his high roller clientele from around the world came for their 'special sweets,' he laced them with precious stones. Once the diners had stuffed their faces with the grotesque meal, Valjean would offer a laxative and sieve and usher them into the toilet. There, he'd watch as his perverse clients returned from the *pissoirs* beaming with joy having retrieved shit-covered jewels from their privileged arses.

Word spread around the globe's culinary circles about the decadence of Valjean's underground soirees, and the clients he attracted came from a different league altogether. At first, they had been successful businessmen who made their money from banking, stocks and shares, along with show business people and rock stars – all prepared to pay small fortunes for the French chef's disgusting sweets. But as the nights at Valjean's restaurant became ever-more notorious for their eliteness, so did his clientele. Soon, the restaurant began attracting kings, queens, maharajahs, sheiks, and the billionaires who actually ran the world – not the poxy puppet governments – the *real* power.

Over the next few years, the gatherings grew and grew. Not with the number of attendees, oh, no, each night would only ever entertain 12 guests. The gatherings grew in notoriety, they grew in intensity, they grew in debauchery, they grew in hate, they grew in selfishness, they grew in self-indulgence, and they grew in absurdity as the levels of decency were pushed and stretched all out of proportion until there was no humanity left in that quaint little restaurant by the sea.

Before long, the clientele had become so elite that no amount of money could buy a ticket. It didn't matter who you were, how rich and powerful, it was strictly by invitation only. Valjean had his pick of the world's most famous and rich, which he eventually turned into a lottery. It cost a cool one million Euros just to be entered into the draw to be considered – and Valjean routinely sold over a hundred tickets for each assembly.

As for the courses themselves, they became more and more obscene as diners were even given the chance to slaughter the animal of their choice if they so wished, which made it quite *sacrificial*. It was culinary depravity at its most base level, and guests could order whatever their depraved palates desired, however obscure. A most popular dish was human flesh carved from freshly executed death row prisoners.

Valjean rarely made any visits to Marius. If he did, it was only out of necessity to deliver the poor wretch's food – always tinned with no labels. Marius had no idea what each meal was going to be until he opened the can; one night it might be peaches, another, dog food. Occasionally, if Valjean was drunk enough, he would throw some horse meat down the cellar stairs, and Marius and Dog would dine like imaginary kings.

One night, the restaurant's clientele was entirely made up of wealthy Asian bankers. They'd requested a dish to remind them of home, so Valjean paid an unsolicited visit to the cellar whilst Marius and Dog were sleeping. There, he grabbed a bottle of wine from one of the racks of countless Riojas and Merlots with one hand and the lead attached to Dog's collar with the other. As he dragged Dog up the stairs to the sound of the wretched animal's dry honks, Marius awoke. Alas, he was too late to stop his brother from taking Dog to his doom.

Marius banged and thumped upon that heavy wooden door for hours until his fists were raw and bleeding. He screamed his protestations through the night until he lost his stunted voice altogether. Then, exhausted, he drank 2 bottles of red wine and passed out.

He came to a few hours later sitting on the high-backed throne where Valjean would sit to play Master of Ceremonies, holding court on his special evenings' proceedings. Marius wore a cowl of some sort and felt something dripping onto his face.

Valjean made his poor brother dance on the table for the guests and sing one of his hit records over and over again. It was a song Marius had heard his brother sing countless times through the floor as a small child. Then, Valjean made his brother howl his way through *No Regrets* while running the gauntlet of the fat, rich fucks spitting and shouting "freak" at him as he danced by, kicking the plates of food as he went.

It was only when Marius slipped on some spilled wine and fell flat onto his back that he saw what had been dripping on him. There, hanging above, was Dog. His only friend had been skinned and gutted and crucified on the restaurant's ceiling. The cowl Marius wore was Dog's face, and the animal's bloodied pelt clung to his naked back like a gruesome hoodie.

Marius felt a rage burning inside of him, something so deep from a place he'd been cultivating for so long – and it was finally set free.

Grabbing a steak knife from the table, in the blink of an eye, Marius slit the throat of the closest Asian businessman.

Panicked, the others scrambled to their feet and jostled Marius to the floor. Knife still clenched in his hand, Marius lashed out and sliced through the Achilles tendons of 3 of his brother's guests with one vicious swipe. The trio dropped to the floor clutching their ankles while their associates ran in blind panic to the restaurant's thick steel door. Of course, the door was securely locked; the one and only electronic key was in Valjean's pocket, and he was motionless in a state of shock.

Ignoring the screams of pain and panic around him, Marius calmly picked up a copper ladle from the floor, walked over to his brother, who was frantically trying to retrieve the key fob from his pocket, and smashed the heavy spoon square into his face. The ladle connected with a loud, wet *crack*, shattering Valjean's nose and knocking him unconscious – he slumped lifeless from his chair.

Marius then turned around and systematically executed each one of the guests with the ladle and steak knife. Naturally, he felt nothing because everything to him was a *documentary* – just like he'd seen a thousand times on that old black and white TV down in the cellar.

In his twisted mind, Marius thought that maybe, one day, he might be in a documentary all of his own, so he cleaned up the mess and hid the corpses of the Asian businessmen in the giant walk-in fridge that housed all the precious meats. Diligently, quietly, Marius mopped up the puddles of blood and took Dog down from the ceiling. He laid his best friend's ruined body on his bed and covered it with his only blanket.

Marius then took the wicker chair he had in the cellar up to the dining room, stripped his brother naked, and tied him to it.

He'd always been told that, should he cut himself cleaning up, he ought never use plasters because they could end up in the food. Instead, he must use Superglue to close any cuts. With that in mind, Marius went into the store cupboard, opened a drawer, and grabbed a small, metallic tube.

He then proceeded to glue Valjean's lips together.

Then each eyelid.

That done, Marius strapped his brother's ankles and wrists to the rattan chair with plastic cable ties and sat down in front of him to wait for him to awaken.

It wasn't too long before Valjean came to. He could barely breathe, and panic set in when he realised he couldn't open his mouth and eyes. Breathing heavily through his smashed nose, he snorted splinters of cartilage and bone into his lungs, along with blood and mucus from his fractured face....

Marius laughed and laughed and began bleaching the room. He thought Valjean might die, or he might live – he cared neither way, and went off to bed. There, he laid next to Dog's remains fully expecting Valjean to be dead by morning.

But no.

Upon investigation the next morning, Valjean was still breathing.

What was Marius to do?

He thought long and hard about the documentary unfolding before him. What would the viewers want to see?

Eventually, it came to him. He knew exactly what to do. It was 28 days before the next gathering of the world's decadent elite, and Marius would give them an experience of a lifetime, one well worth a million dollars of anyone's money. His brilliant idea would win awards for its contribution to television.

And so, for the next 28 days, Marius minced the remains of the Asian businessmen, mixed them up with some gold leaf, rice, and maize, and ground it all into a mushy pulp. For good measure, he added a generous amount of Napoleon brandy. Four times a day, Marius inserted a plastic tube into one of his brother's nostrils all the way down to his stomach. He'd then pump the protein and fat-rich gloop directly into Valjean's gut.

Valjean struggled against the intrusion each time. He'd try to force his glued mouth open to scream and used the tiny muscles in his closed eyelids to let Marius see the fear in them. But, with only one nostril clear, Valjean could never get enough oxygen into his lungs and would black out at every sitting.

In reality, that was a blessing in disguise.

Every time the rich gloop was administered, Valjean would struggle, writhe, and buck in that wicker chair, but he was getting weaker by the day. By the end of the second week, he'd given up fighting and just took it. He'd gained four stone in that time, was fat and bloated. His bulging veins showed through his translucent, greasy skin, sweat oozed constantly from his pores, and blood seeped from the corners of his mouth and eyes. Pneumonia had begun to take a hold because shards of bone and some of Marius' gloop had made it into his lungs, and they filled with fluid. He'd suffer violent coughing fits, during which he'd hack up blood and nasty, green mucus through his nose.

Rather thoughtfully, Marius had cut a hole in the seat of the wicker chair to allow Valjean to defecate into a bucket he'd placed directly below. He didn't want the place to stink of shit – he'd had quite enough of that living down in the cellar. Plus, when the cameras arrived to film his documentary, Marius wanted them to think he was a clean boy.

On the morning of Day 28, Marius shaved Valjean's entire body and head using an open blade, cut-throat razor, taking great care not to nick his skin. Then, he dried off his brother's sweat and covered him in gold leaf. He tied a black cable tie around the end of Valjean's circumcised penis and pulled it tight to stop any urine leaving his bladder – he finished off his masterpiece by inserting a large ruby in the eye of Valjean's cock!

The guests were to arrive in just 12 hours, and they'd be expecting something special. Marius was determined to make sure those expectations were more than satisfied. He wanted Valjean to be sweet and tender for his consumers, and so, every two hours, he force-fed a bottle of the sweetest red wine into Valjean's oesophagus. His brother's belly swelled with each bottle, and after every litre was ingested, Marius delighted at the gurgling screams coming from Valjean's nostrils.

It made him smile.

Eventually, the guests did arrive.

They were greeted by Marius wearing one of his twin brother's gold lame stage suits with the cowl of Dog's skin draped over his head and down his back. He ushered all twelve diners in, all the while grinning with his half mouth. The guests were hushed with reverence as they walked into the dining room to be greeted by the bloated, shapeless form at the end of the table. It sat in a wicker chair, its corpulent body draped in a blood-stained shower curtain.

Everyone sat in silence as Marius made his way over to the wicker chair. Grabbing the corner of the curtain, he slowly pulled it away to reveal his twin brother.

There came an audible gasp from the epicurists as they beheld the living, golden effigy displayed before them. Marius held a finger to his disfigured lips to *shhh* them as he cut the cable tie that held Valjean's right arm. He placed the cut-throat razor into his brother's hand....

Valjean shook as he brought the razor up to his left eye and sliced into the lid. The keen, glinting blade cut through the eyelid and deep into his cornea; blood flowed into his eye to blind him. The partially severed lid flapped down onto the mottled, sallow skin of Valjean's cheek and he screamed through his nose as he sliced the blade into his sealed lips. As the agonised, piercing shriek escaped from his throat, the diners got to their feet and applauded.

Encouraged by the approval, Marius began howling *No Regrets* as Valjean severed the end of his own penis with the open razor to free the fluid from his bulging abdomen.

Everyone cheered their utmost respect as Marius plunged a sharpened wine tap into Valjean's jugular vein and filled each of their wine glasses with the sweet, viscous nectar that gushed out.

Each of the twelve raised their glass in a silent toast before gorging themselves on Valjean's blood like the vampires they were becoming.

Marius snatched the blade from Valjean's limp hand and slit open his brother's gut chest to navel. He rummaged around in his brother's steaming body cavity a moment or two before pulling out the engorged, fat-filled liver.

He threw the blood-soaked organ onto the table, and, as his elite guests ate it raw, they bit and scratched and clawed at each other like carrion crows around roadkill.

Marius climbed up onto the table. He picked up a hallmarked, solid silver platter, looked at his reflection, and howled the last verse of the song he'd always sung with his brother.

Non, rien de rien,
Non je ne regrette rien,
Car ma vie, car mes joies,
Ajhourd'hui ca commence avec toi.

Of course, the privileged guests had no idea what Marius was singing – but he certainly did, and that was all that mattered.

Absolutely nothing,
I regret nothing,
Because my life, my joys, today they begin with you.

Marius took a bow to the blood-covered diners, who screamed and clapped their approval at his performance and the gastronomic delight he'd prepared for them.

And it was at that moment that Marius Le Noir knew he was going to be a star.

The Spinster

"So… is this your first time at one of these?" asked Spike. His real name was Malcolm, but he felt *Spike* had a bit more of an edge. Besides, it would make him harder to trace.

Of course, he knew her answer would be a lie, 'cos he *always* lied if someone asked him that same question. He was 57, married with 3 kids, and still reasonably fit and good looking for his age. He took pride in the fact he hadn't lost his hair, even though it was a bit salt and pepper – more salt than pepper, actually. He still considered himself a bit of a catch, and let it be known he felt that way to anyone on his radar.

Malcolm – sorry, *Spike* – had been speed dating before; twelve times, in fact. He was quite the regular at such events, but never in the same town. He'd scour the Internet looking for anything within a 50-mile radius, and would leave his wedding ring in the ash tray of his car. He'd tell his wife he was out with the lads, and had never failed at getting a shag at the end of the night. A quick bunk-up in the local Premier Inn, and he'd be back home by 1 a.m. with his long-suffering wife none the wiser.

However, his run of successful dates was proving more difficult on that particular night. All the other guys there were much younger than him, better looking, had darker hair, and carried less weight. For once, he didn't feel like the 'catch of the night.' Spike had a knack of knowing instantly if he stood a chance with a woman the second he sat down opposite them, and thus far he'd had no luck whatsoever.

She was the last one on the list – he'd gone through 17 potential dates that night and drawn a blank on every one of them. So, this was his last-ditch effort to get his dick wet. In fairness, he'd been watching her out the corner of his eye all night. He thought she appeared closer to his age, which meant none of the *woke* shit, no *don't call me darlin'* or *love* bullshit. You just couldn't say *anything* anymore.

The last couple of women Spike had spoken to had bored him shitless. One even had spinach stuck in her teeth after gorging herself on the free buffet during the 15-minute break – she'd obviously stocked up well on the veggie vol au vents. She also reeked of spaghetti, even though there was none on the buffet. He'd later found out during their chat that she washed her hair in pasta water because she didn't believe in shampoo, animal testing, and all that bollocks. She'd said, "It gives it more volume, too." She'd shouted that, trying to be funny.

She wasn't.

The next one's name tag declared she was called…

Tabitha.

Who the fuck is called *Tabitha* in fucking Swansea?!

Spike always found it amazing how 5 minutes can seem like a fucking lifetime when you're trapped talking to a millennial who rants on about pronouns.

"My ex-boyfriend identifies as a 'she' now and wants a vagina. Good for *her*, I say. Personally, I like to put myself out there as non-binary nowadays!" Tabitha went on.

Spike waited for her to stop talking to catch her breath, smiled at her, and said, "According to Marks and Spencer's sticky toffee pudding, I'm a family of four!" He grinned and waited for a laugh that never came.

"Fucking dinosaur!" she snarled as she got up and went to the next table.

As Spike sat there on his own for a few moments waiting for the last possible date of the night, his mind drifted off. He thought that maybe, sometime in the distant future, an alien archeologist from Alpha Centauri would conclude that, in the first half of the 21st century, humans had suddenly stopped talking to each other – stopped *communicating* – fearful of causing offence or attracting prosecution and imprisonment. Instead, they all just sat in silence, masturbating alone, and eventually died out. Perhaps it'll be for the best, Spike mused.

His thoughts were interrupted as the woman he'd had his eye on sat down opposite and smiled. She plonked a pint of lager down on the table, smiled at him, and said, "You're my last one, apparently."

"You're mine too," Spike replied with a smile. She was so much prettier than he'd first thought upon spotting her earlier. She had long, thick, jet-black hair that fell to just below her slender shoulders. It had a few odd strands of grey that gave the impression of a small, white river running down a mountainside, and there was not even a hint of pasta smell. Her voice was soft with an accent he couldn't quite place, but she spoke with purpose.

The woman seemed very confidant, and her green eyes caught him by surprise – they immediately drew him in. They were all he could focus on.

Fuck me. There's definitely *something about this one*, he thought. If love at first sight was a real thing, it was happening to him right there and then.

"So… is this your first time at one of these?"

"No."

Fuck, thought Spike, *she didn't lie!*

"I come to these things a lot," the woman admitted. "What about you? I'll bet you're an old hand."

"Yes… bloody right I am!" Spike shocked himself at how candid he was. He then looked deeply into those gorgeous green eyes and said, "I've never not had a shag at the end of one of these!"

What the fuck?! Spike's brain screamed at him. *Shut up, you twat!*

She paused, smiled again, and asked, "Are you married?"

"Yep," Spike replied nonchalantly. Once again, he couldn't believe what was happening: for the first time in his life, he was telling the *truth* to a woman he intended to fuck. He just couldn't hold back.

"Kids?" She spoke softly with seduction in her voice.

"Three of them – 9, 12, and 17. Every one of 'em a pain in the fucking arse." He had no filter! Looking away from the woman's eyes, disbelieving what was happening, Spike was determined not to look at her and to get back to his lying ways. But, the second she spoke, he *had* to look into those eyes again.

"I take it your wife doesn't know about your extracurricular activities?"

"No. Stupid bitch doesn't have a clue." Spike felt angry at himself – angry and *confused*. He was confused by his answers and confused by the woman's response to every question. She didn't seem put off by his truths at all. In fact, she appeared to be enjoying the fact he was being so open.

I need to take control of this – it's getting out of hand, thought Spike.

Listening to the woman's voice, he noticed her accent again. He *still* couldn't place it, but everything else about her distracted him: her eyes, the way she looked at him, her hair, and especially her *smell*. It was like something he'd seen on a David Attenborough documentary years ago. What was it? Love? Lust? Pheromones? Or could it have been that he hadn't had sex – or even a wank – for over a week?

"You're not from around here, are you?" he asked, laughing to himself at how unoriginal the question was.

"Oh, can you tell?" She said as Spike looked at her name tag. It read, *Ragno*. He then looked back into her mesmerising green eyes and opened his mouth to speak.

"It's Italian. *I'm* Italian." She anticipated his question. "I'm from Naples." She then smiled at Spike and he was gone, utterly transfixed. He was so drawn in, it was unbelievable. Something in the back of his mind lit a fire in his bonce: *Ragno? I read about that word once? What did that mean? I've definitely heard it somewhere before… never mind, it'll come back to me later.*

"Are *you* married?" Spike blurted out, hoping against hope she wasn't.

"No," she replied. "I'm a spinster."

"*Spinster*?" laughed Spike. "That's a bit dated, isn't it?"

"What can I say?" said Ragno with an enigmatic smile. I'm just an old-fashioned kind of girl."

Spike wasn't sure if she'd just winked at him or not – and then he caught her scent.

Oh, fucking God!

She had the fragrance of Heaven: a heady mix of her sex, her love, and everything he'd ever wanted in just one small intake of breath….

Spkie sat in open-mouthed awe of the unbelievable woman only 2 feet away from him. Seizing the moment, he leant forward and kissed her plump, luscious lips. Ragno didn't back away, so Spike flicked his tongue into her mouth. He heard her respond with an almost imperceptible moan from the very back of her throat, and then she slipped her tongue into his mouth – but more forcefully than he'd done to her. It took Spike by surprise, but in a very good way, indeed.

The incredible moment was broken by the sound of the Klaxon from the bar.

That's it!" shouted the landlord. "Time's up! Last date and last orders – bar shuts in 5 minutes. Thanks for coming, everyone. The next *New Romantics Speedate* night is 4 weeks from now – on the 20th of August."

"Wanna get out of here?" Spike asked.

Ragno smiled at him again. She nodded.

Oh, God, I'm in love! he thought.

Picking up her handbag, Ragno fished out her phone. "Smile!" she said and snapped him on her iPhone. "Just a little souvenir for me." With a cheeky wink, she took Spike's hand and led him to the door.

"I've got a room at a hotel not far from here," Spike told her.

"No," she said firmly. "I don't do hotels. My house is only a couple of miles away. I assume you have a car?"

"Uh huh."

"Leave it here. I'll drop you back… after."

Wow! thought Spike. *Top-quality shag* and *chauffeur-driven as well!*

Ragno led him to a brand-new, black Tesla with blacked-out windows. "Fuck me sideways," Spike murmured quietly to himself. His new friend heard him and smiled once again.

With a motor like that, the Italian woman must have some dough to her name, Spike thought. *Bingo!*

"Gotta do my bit for the environment." Ragno rummaged around in her handbag and pulled out the fancy key fob. She pressed the button and the car lit up like a computer from the 1960's. It reminded Spike of his favourite childhood TV show, *The Time Tunnel*, in which two intrepid travellers – Doug and Tony – jumped from one famous event in history to another. Each episode dropped them right into the heart of the action, whether on the deck of the Titanic on its maiden voyage, the battle of Agincourt, or Hiroshima just before the bomb dropped. Of course, they'd be pulled out each week just in the nick of time – only to find themselves in yet another sticky situation. Literally out of the frying pan and into the fire. They never landed anywhere nice – like in a Tesla with the most gorgeous, sexy woman on the planet. *Ah. Doug and Tony – what a pair of tossers*, Spike thought to himself as he climbed into Ragno's car.

She touched a slender finger to the keyless ignition, and the electric car left the pub's car park in complete silence.

Spike surreptitiously slid a hand into the coin pocket of his jeans and plucked out a small, blue pill. He gulped it down dry. Spike may have thought of himself as a catch, but he still needed that extra bit of insurance.

He thought his actions had gone unnoticed, but no – the woman clocked everything. Spike never said a word on the short journey to Ragno's house because he was worried the honesty trip he was be on might hinder his chances of a happy ending to the evening.

He needn't have worried.

Ragno held her silence while driving. She, too, never said a single word. Every now, though, she shot her passenger a sultry smile and rested a hand upon his knee for a second or two whilst waiting for a red light to change. That gentle touch was enough for Spike to feel the little blue pill take effect.

The journey took no more than 15 minutes. The Tesla glided silently to halt outside an archway in an old flint wall that must've reached at least 10-feet high. Spike noted they'd been driving down a winding country lane for about mile and the wall stretched the entire length of it. Ragno turned the car off and cracked open the door; the interior light flicked on. Then, she turned in her seat, swung her feet out of the car and onto the road, then turned her head to face him. "You coming?"

Bloody right I'm coming! thought Spike. He tried to stay cool and just nodded, but the bulge in his pants gave away his true impatience. Once again, the woman noticed everything.

Ragno closed the Tesla's door quietly, and the interior lights went out. That left Spike fumbling for his door handle in the dark. He found it eventually, but still hadn't opened the door by the time Ragno walked around to the other side of the car and opened it for him.

"I couldn't get out," whined Spike.

"Child locks." She grinned as she took his hand to help him out the car. He was desperate to hide his growing erection.

"So, you *do* have kids?" Spike sounded disapproving.

"No," replied Ragno. "It's just for safety."

"Safety?"

"Yes, that's all."

Ragno led Spike under the flint archway and by some old outbuildings that might have once been cowsheds; it was difficult to tell in the darkness. The two walked for a few minutes, with Spike happy to be led blindly by the beautiful woman he'd only just met along a gravel pathway. The crunching of tiny stones beneath their feet disturbed the shrill baying of mating foxes somewhere in the distance.

Suddenly, the clouds drifted and the yellowed moon lit up the silhouette of a house a little way ahead. Only one room was illuminated – there was a faint yellow glow coming from the hallway window.

"Careful, now," said Ragno as she guided Spike up the small, stone step to the front door. "We don't want any accidents."

As Ragno stepped up to the door, it opened without her touching it. Turning around, she started walking backwards into the hallway, leading Spike inside.

Spike saw the yellow glow in the hallway was coming from a huge candle. It was the sort they have in old Catholic churches. Not that he'd been in one for years, but he'd seen them on telly on Christmas services – or perhaps it was on *Stars on Sunday*? – back when he was a kid.

The door closed behind them – once again, of its own accord – and Spike's nostrils flared as he caught the strong smell of some kind of incense.

Oh, fuck, he thought. *Here comes my fucking allergies.* At that, Spike began to sneeze uncontrollably.

As Ragno tossed her head back and laughed hard, Spike felt his erection quickly dissipate. And, once again, the woman noticed everything. It made her laugh even more.

"It is an acquired aroma, isn't it?" Ragno chuckled.

Spike nodded and realized it was a blend of what he had smelled on Ragno during their speed date plus something else….

What was that? Moth balls? Formaldehyde? Or something long-dead? He shrugged it off, pissed off that his rock-hard knob had evaporated and he couldn't hide his frustration.

Eventually, Spike's sneezing fit died down. It was then he noticed the walls of the hallway were lined with photographs of men. Dozens upon dozens of them. Some were very old sepia photos framed in black oak, others more modern. They spanned the length of the hallway from the front door and seemed to follow a timeline from the early 1800's right up to the present.

"Who the fuck are these guys?" Spike scanned the pictures. His back to his date, he sensed her move towards him and felt the warmth of her body against his. He then saw, reflected in the glass of one of photos, someone – *something* –

who wasn't Ragno….

Before Spike had a chance to react and turn round, he felt a sharp stabbing pain in his neck.

He passed out instantly.

Spike had no idea how long he was knocked out for. It was still dark when he awoke with a pounding headache. He saw through the leaded windows of the room he was in that the moon was still out, albeit hidden behind the fluffy clouds. He reckoned he could've been out for a few minutes, a few hours… longer?

He had no idea he'd been stone-cold unconscious for 3 days.

Spike wasn't actually *cold*. It was just the opposite, in fact – he was burning up. He also couldn't move. He was paralysed! He tried to move a hand, a foot, even a finger or two, but nothing happened.

Panic began to set in when Spike realised he was hanging upside down by his feet with blood rushing to his head to pound his brain.

In the pitch darkness, the yellow glow from a flickering candle approached from the other side of the room. It illuminated enough for him to see he was in a very long drawing room of sorts.

As the dancing flame approached, Spike strained his eyes to see Ragno holding the candle. She was entirely naked. He was shocked to realise he still fancied her and *still* wanted the shag he'd been expecting. He was tied upside down, and yet his erection defied gravity to stand out at a painfully stiff 45-degree angle from his own completely naked body.

Ragno placed the candle on the floor in front of Spike. He looked up at his suspended body to see he wasn't really paralysed at all: he was cocooned in some kind of silken mesh with only his dick and balls uncovered. He looked at his date-turned-captor through blood-filled eyes and saw she was smiling at him.

And then she changed.

As Spike watched, Ragno's head split apart and her face fell away. Instead of a human skull behind the peeling flesh, Spike saw what he *thought* he'd seen in the reflection in the glass of the hallway photograph. As the once-beautiful woman's skin and flesh shed away, she tore at it with her fingers, ripping into muscles and sinews, to reveal a bulbous, black head with eight shining, ebony eyes.

Spike couldn't tear his terrified eyes away from the spectacle as, with shredded, discarded flesh lying at her bare feet, Ragno's nude body began to swell, its skin splitting to reveal the horror beneath….

It was then Spike remembered the word.

Ragno.

It had been a general knowledge question on *Who Wants to be a Millionaire* some months before.

It was Italian for *spider*.

As Spike looked into his date's eight eyes for the very last time, she whispered, "I told you I was a spinster."

Mercifully, Spike – *Malcolm* – felt no pain at all as Ragno pierced his scrotum with her fangs and pumped his balls full of venom. She laughed upon seeing his erection disappear one last time.

Annus Horribilis

In 1555, Nostradamus published his book of prophecies. Some thought him insane, some thought him a charlatan, but some thought he knew what he was talking about; in particular, Catharine de Medici, wife of King Henry the II of France. She made him counsellor and physician-in-ordinary to her son, the young king Charles IX.

Over the next 450 years or so, Nostradamus's predictions hung around successive generations and were often resurrected in times of global strife, only to be ultimately dismissed by the majority. Only a few hard-core stalwarts still actually believed, none more than the self-monikered *Annus of Nostradamus* – literally, the *Year of Nostradamus* – a group of radicals that began sabotaging anything they could in an attempt to steer events towards making one of their hero's thousands of prophesies or quatrains ring true.

Formed in the 16th century, not long after Nostradamus died in 1556, the group infiltrated every government organisation in every country. They became a cult of enormous subterfuge, even worming their way into the Vatican. There, they reached the ranks of the 12 bishops who personally served the pope as his successor. Even to this day, one of their legion sits in the pope's chair.

The *Annus of Nostradamus* had a hand in every war in history. They nudged every little nuance they could to fit their agenda: Archduke Franz Ferdinand was assassinated by one of their associates, as were the Kennedys, Lennon, Princess Diana, the Ghandis, Martin Luther King, William McKinley, James Garfield… Abraham Lincoln was an exception – he had far too many enemies anyway. Nonetheless, John Wilkes Boothe was taken down by the *Annus*.

They also infiltrated royal families through marriage:

The House of Saxe Coburg and Tothas – Belgium.

The House of Bernadotte – Sweden.

The House of Borbon Anjou – Spain.

The House of Windsor – United Kingdom.

The House of Liechtenstein.

The House of Luxembourg.

The list is endless….

It was all done in plain sight, of course, right under the very noses of those the *Annus* chose to permeate. And yet, they didn't see it.

They should've done.

Hindsight is a rare gift very few possess, but if we *really* look back, there are patterns to be seen every step of the way.

The *Annus* had scientists working with Robert Oppenheimer on the Manhattan Project. Once the United States discovered the Germans were mining uranium in the early 1940's, the *Annus* pushed for the Americans to step up their efforts to produce the atom bomb first. While the world tuned in to the theatre of war on their transistor radios, they were blissfully unaware the project was leading mankind into a brand-new age, a nuclear age, where the splitting of just one atom of uranium would set in motion a chain reaction of unimaginably devastating consequences for the entire human race.

They called the first experiments 'tickling the dragon's tail,' and had the western world cheering their victories and mourning the wounds of their defeats. Then, in the New Mexico desert on the 16th of July, 1945, the dragon breathed its first breath as the Americans tested the atom bomb, Trinity. The blast created a mushroom cloud over 40,000-feet high and ushered in the evil shadow of nuclear war.

A few weeks later, Germany surrendered, but the Americans – still pressing for Japan's unconditional surrender – dropped the bomb anyway. Even though the war was all but over, that fearsome dragon breathed fire and devastation in Hiroshima. Again, just 3 days later, it took its second breath in Nagasaki, and Robert Oppenheimer became the instrument of the destroyer of worlds.

And so it continued. The *Annus* had a strong, powerful foothold in the rise of the nuclear age, and, by 1949, the Russians had the atom bomb – courtesy of the followers of Nostradamus.

During the course of the next half century, another 6 nations followed suit:

United Kingdom – 1952.

France – 1960.

China – 1964.

India – 1974.

Pakistan – 1998.

North Korea – 2006.

All courtesy of the *Annus of Nostradamus*.

Nostradamus had predicted each one of those events in history. To him, they were the future, and as time progressed, his final prediction for the end of mankind was growing closer and closer....

The global COVID-19 pandemic of 2019 was blamed on a virus jumping from infected bats at a wet market in Wuhan, China. It was glaringly obvious it had nothing to do with bats and the Chinese peoples' eating habits, but the propaganda machine was in full flow – spearheaded by the disciples of Nostradamus, the see'er.

Not long after COVID-19 began, the brutal curtain of war lifted once again as Russia invaded Ukraine in an attempt to reassemble the old Soviet Union. Vladimir Putin's advisors were all sympathisers of the *Annus*, who were as firmly entrenched in Russia as Grigori Rasputin – himself, a lord of their ranks – in the late 19th and early 20th century. Rasputin was confidante and advisor to Nicholas II, the last emperor of Russia, and had considerable influence in the empire. He was eventually assassinated in 1916 after an almost-fatal stabbing failed to kill him in 1913. He was poisoned by cyanide – twice – and both attempts failed.

So, they shot him in the back.

Rasputin then raised himself from the dead some few hours later, only to be shot in the back of the head at close range and his body dumped in the river. He supposedly drowned. However, rumours spread that Rasputin came back once more, only to finally succumb to typhoid in 1921. He was a disciple of the highest degree, maybe even of Satan himself.

Much like the Manhattan Project in the 1940's was shrouded in secrecy to mask its true objectives, so was the LHC – the Large Hadron Collider. It was built underground by CERN on the border between France and Switzerland. Thousands teams of scientists from countless different countries were involved – all headed by members of the *Annus*.

The LHC stretched 17 miles in circumference and was first tested in 2008. Ostensibly, its purpose was to search for unknown dimensions and the smallest sub-atomic particle thought to exist: the Higgs Boson – the fabled *God Particle*.

Detecting the Higgs Boson was to be achieved by firing two protons – one from each end of the giant, cylindrical tube – directly at each other. In doing so, it was calculated that, during the ensuing subatomic explosion, the smallest particle known to man would be discovered. That would change forever how the scientific world viewed practically *everything* in the universe.

Of course, there were possible side effects to the endeavour: by performing the experiment, it was hypothesised a small black hole on Earth could be created. Such a body would suck everything in our solar system in to oblivion and, in effect, create a doorway to another dimension. Naturally, the theory was pooh-poohed as utter nonsense by the CERN scientists, and anyone of any note who dared pay attention to it was discredited.

But, the *Annus* knew exactly what it was doing.

It wasn't a black hole that could be created, it wasn't a doorway – it was a *bridge*.

A bridge that had never been crossed before.

On Christmas Eve, 2029, the CERN boffins discovered precisely what they were looking for. Two protons smashed into each other at almost the speed of light to create the tiniest of explosions, undetectable to the naked eye. Nonetheless, the vast array of sensors and computers detected the anomaly, and the world's press were there to witness it.

The proton collision itself was quite uneventful. It was simply a blip on a monitor and a flashing green light.

As insignificant as it may have seemed, that blip and tiny green flash signalled the beginning of the end because, in that moment, a singularity on Earth was conceived. Within that singularity, the laws of physics broke down and a black hole was born. Not only had CERN tickled the dragon's tail, its wings were fully extended and it was airborne.

All ready to begin the task of consuming the entire planet.

That green light kept on flashing, and the hundreds of white-coated conspirators cheered and raised their glasses to one another. It was close to midnight and, as the digital clock changed to 12.01 a.m., they wished themselves a very merry Christmas – blissfully unaware the God particle they'd been searching for actually had very little do with God.

Inadvertently, they had opened the gateway to what some may call Heaven or Hell. There really is no distinction. It was the place we humans had searched for since we first walked upon the Earth: life after death.

However, it was not simply life after death. The place CERN discovered was also life *before* birth. Science has proved there is a finite amount of energy in the universe, which cannot be created nor destroyed – it can only transform from one form into another.

So, in the moment of the pair of protons' collision, every fragment of energy that has ever existed found its way into our world. Every living thing that ever lived and died emerged, everything that had just been waiting for a window found its way into our dimension… and those energies required living hosts to inhabit so they could be alive once again. Some had been dead a long, long time and had waited almost an eternity for their time back on the carousel they knew as *life*.

Of course, the dead far outweigh the living – there were 10 billion people on earth in 2029 and 100 billion ghosts behind them. And so, the souls of the dead took over every single human in one fell swoop – 10-fold – to live again. So many invading souls was far too much for human minds to deal with, and every person felt their own soul drown among the legion inhabiting each and every one of them.

The old souls' hunger for life took on the unprecedented surge of ancient malevolence that had remained dormant for eons. The only things separating humans from animals was the ability to think, to reason, to understand, to empathise, and once those things were taken away, all Hell broke loose.

Literally.

A gruesome feeding frenzy took place; the scientists and journalists in the LHC compound tore each other apart with bare hands, ripped limbs from still-screaming bodies, and devoured each other. And, once they had fed, the strongest ones who had survived that first orgy of cannibalism began eating themselves. Then, with no limbs left, they wriggled toward anything else left alive and ate the faces of the corpses surrounding them.

Finally, they expired, screaming into the deaf-mute world the Earth had become.

The 100 billion spores of the virus that was the long dead spread instantaneously across the globe, and the human race was gone in a space of 12 hours. There was no lockdown, no W.H.O. warning, no vaccination….

There was nothing.

We were the virus, and the Earth finally breathed a sigh of relief as the dragon took its last breath.

***

I write this in the past tense, for I have seen all of it happen. But you have not – because it hasn't happened *yet*.

I am writing this myself in 1554 – not long before the annus of my death.

The Living Room

"So... do you know why it's called a 'wake'?" Asked the grizzled old man with yellow eyes. He smelled of some pungent 1970's aftershave and wore a tailcoat dinner suit that had seen better days – it looked like it belonged in a museum of antiquities as an homage to what Fred Astaire might've worn in the 30's. The old man's accent was RP with just a tinge of Norfolk to it.

"What?" said Greg.

"I said –" retorted the old man.

"I know what you said," snapped Greg. "I fucking heard you."

"Well, you just said *what*, so I thought I'd best repeat the question," the old man said. "What about 'his face rings a bell'? Do you know where that one comes from? It doesn't have to be the end, you know!"

"What the fuck are you talking about?"

"And... more importantly –"

"Who the bloody 'ell are you?" Greg snarled. "She's only been in a coffin in the ground for 5 hours, and you're asking me fucking stupid questions!" Greg shook with anger, frustration, fear, and every emotion one feels when the light of their life is extinguished.

"Do you know why it's called the 'living room'?" The old man smirked. "Should really be called the 'dying room' when you think about it – don't you think? It was, after all, in this very room she died, wasn't it?!"

Jenny had been 22 years younger than Greg. He'd been married before, and they'd joke about it whenever Greg introduced her to his friends as his 2nd wife. She would counter by saying he was her *first* husband and she would out live him by years. Then it would be her turn to find a boy toy.

But no, that wasn't gonna happen now.

Greg loved her, *really* loved her.

They'd moved from Guildford, Surrey to Norfolk only 18 months earlier. After the move, Jenny became distant, and Greg thought she might be having an affair.

But it was worse than that, much worse....

After Jenny was diagnosed with cancer, Greg gave up work after 26 years in the police force – he was a sergeant – to take care of her. Sadly, she faded fast.

And then she was gone.

The old man started talking again. "It's called a 'wake' because, after the great plague of London in 1665, people would lay the recently deceased in a room and sit and watch to see if they would wake up before they buried them. Back then, a lot of people fell into comas through lead poisoning from the pots and pans and drinking mugs. And... that's why it's a called a 'wake'."

Greg just stared at the man. He felt his anger building. He wasn't shaking – it wasn't *that* visible – he was more *vibrating* than anything.

Everyone had left – apart from the old man.

Greg had no idea where he'd come from – or who the Hell he was – he just knew he wanted him to shut up.

"'Your face rings a bell' comes from the same period. People who weren't actually dead were often buried during the plague. They'd pile coffin on top of coffin on top of coffin because they were running out of space in London. When they dug a hole to put in another coffin, the gravediggers would see scratch marks on the inside of some of the older ones – they were burying people *alive*! So, in the end they put little bells in with the bodies. If a 'dead body' woke up, they'd just ring their bell in the hope someone passing would hear and dig them out. Stupid bastards – what they needed was a living room!"

Greg punched the old man hard and fast. *Crack!* Straight on the nose. The old man recoiled, but only slightly. A single bead of blood dripped from each nostril. He slowly took out a yellowing handkerchief from his top pocket and dabbed at the claret.

"I don't think *that* was necessary," whispered the old man with a grin.

Greg stood frozen in shock and guilt for punching such a frail remnant of a man. He also felt intrigue as to why the old boy was still standing. Greg had done a little boxing on the force as a younger man, and a punch like that ought to have fucked *anyone* six ways from Sunday.

That said, the old codger not only stood his ground, but he looked as if he were smiling at Greg.

"I'm sorry," Stammered Greg, "I shouldn't have done that."

"No, you shouldn't," said the old man.

"Do you want help?" Greg asked as the trickle of blood from the man's nose became thicker from one nostril and started to flow slowly like thin, red lava onto his top lip.

Instead of dabbing at it, the old man flicked his tongue along the ridge of his lip. He tasted the blood, *savoured* it. He closed his eyes as he brought his tongue back into his mouth to suck at the muscle and swallow hard; it was as if he was drinking a fine, fortified wine.

Greg took a step back. He couldn't hide the look of disgust on his face at the old man's actions. He caught another whiff of the man's aftershave – he'd smelled it before, and it smelled of *old*. His dad used to wear it, and there was no mistaking the 'great smell of Brut.' It was like surgical alcohol mixed with homemade rose petal perfume and a touch of toilet cleaner. Immensely popular in its day. Now, not so much.

"Oh, I'm *so* sorry," said the old man. "I forgot you are in a state of mourning. I do apologise. Let me tell you who I am and why I'm here."

"Yes, I think you should," said Greg. "I've never seen you before in my life. Did you come here straight after the funeral? Did you know Jen? Are you a relative? *Who the fuck are you?*"

"No." The old man spoke softly. "I'm not a relative. I never knew your wife. My name is Cecil. I don't have a surname, or should I say, I don't *remember* my family name. I work for Lord Sax Vandenburgh – he's second cousin to the late queen. Victoria, that is, not Elizabeth. His land backs onto the nice little garden you have here. If you look over that hedge, you may just see the edge of Hockham Hall. It's over there, behind that little coppice of trees. I planted them myself, I did. I've been in his service for over 150 years now."

"Do you want another punch on the fucking nose?" Angry, Greg stepped closer to the old man.

"Please," said Cecil. "That's *really* not necessary. Lord Vandenburgh heard about your wife's passing, and, as you must've found out, village life is somewhat of a microcosm compared to big city life. Through the village grapevine, he found out about your previous life as a member of the constabulary – the Lord is a big fan of the Peelers, as he likes to call them. What I'm trying to say is that Lord Vandenburgh wants to help."

"How the fuck can he help when Jen's already dead and in the ground?" Greg growled. "What the fuck can he do for me? Give me a job milking his fucking cows?"

"That's just it," Cecil replied. "It doesn't have to be the end. Not for your Miss Jenny. I have a personal invite for you from Lord Vandenburgh…" Cecil reached inside his tailcoat jacket and pulled out a black envelope.

He handed it to Greg.

"What's this?" asked Greg.

"Like I said – it's an invite."

"Yes, yes, yes – from fucking Lord Van der Valk."

"*Vandenburgh*," Cecil reprimanded.

"Yes. Well, you've given it to me. Now, *fuck off*, you mentalist." Greg turned the old man round and ushered him out of the front door. Before Greg had a chance to shut the door, Cecil put one finger against the wooden frame to hold it open. Greg put all his weight behind trying to close the door, but it wouldn't budge.

"It doesn't have to be the end," Cecil repeated. "But this offer is not indefinite. It has to be taken up in the next 24 hours or it becomes null and void. Think fast and act quickly, Greg – Lord Vandenburgh is waiting."

Cecil lifted his finger and the door slammed shut.

Greg poured himself a large glass of whisky and downed it in one go. Collapsing onto the sofa, he poured himself another, and then another, and then he fell asleep.

He awoke in the early hours of the morning with the unopened invite on his chest. It was sealed with red wax and stamped with the skull of a goat.

Greg opened the envelope. Inside was a black card embossed in gold leaf. It read:

Lord Jurgen Vandenburgh invites you to the 'living room' in the hall of Great Hockham at the hour of 2 a m.

You must bring with you something the deceased had on them when they died.

This invite expires in 1 day. If you are not here by then, the Great Hall is closed to you.

Forever.

Squinting at his watch through bloodshot eyes and one hell of a headache, Greg saw it was 1.35 a.m.

And he was still drunk.

Hung around Greg's neck was Jen's wedding ring. He kept it on an old leather shoestring. He'd taken it from her finger the afternoon she passed and had worn it ever since. He placed his hand on the ring, closed his fist around it, and began to weep silently.

Greg struggled to his feet and made his way to the double back doors of his house. He then staggered up the garden to the 5ft-high hawthorn bushes that separated his property from the grounds of Hockham Hall.

Pausing for just a moment, Greg pushed his way through the bushes. The jagged thorns tore away at his black Ted Baker suit he'd worn for his wife's funeral earlier in the day. The hawthorns' jagged barbs also cut into his neck and hands, gouging the skin open to leave it raw and bleeding. He felt no pain because the alcohol was like anaesthetic in his blood – but grief was the main numbing agent.

Greg made his way across the open field, waking a few sheep sleeping in his path. He paid no heed to them.

Eventually, he came to the door of the Great Hall. He stood outside the wooden entrance that seemed more like a portcullis. It stretched at least 20-feet high. He pulled at an iron lever, suspecting it was the equivalent of a doorbell.

It never made a sound.

Greg pulled at the lever again and again while banging his other fist on the ancient, dark wood. Then, a small iron-grated panel flipped open.

Cecil's familiar eyes held Greg's gaze for a second. The panel slapped shut.

Greg heard various locks and sliders being turned and pulled until, finally, the huge door opened and Cecil beckoned him in.

"I knew you would come." Smiled Cecil as he pushed the huge door closed with the ease of a child closing a doll's house door. "He's waiting for you in the living room. This way."

Greg followed on silently. He took little notice of his surroundings, but had he been sober, he would've noticed the Gothic Biblical tapestries hung along the old wood-panelled walls. The tapestries depicted countless horrors from Hell: the rising demons, the falling of angels, the despicable tortures meted upon souls in that terrible place. And, above each entrance to the many doors he passed through, a hideous gargoyle perched at the top of the frame.

On a sober day, Greg may even have noticed the pungent smell of burning flesh. But no – not that night: his senses were dulled, his mind was spinning.

Eventually, after passing through myriad rooms, each one as equally as unsettling as the last, Cecil paused and turned to look back at Greg, who stood behind him, swaying.

"You are about to enter the 'living room.' Lord Vandenburgh will help you. You must listen to what he says. You must do as he asks. There, you will find what you are looking for."

Greg nodded slowly as he listened to every word without understanding any of them. "Get out of the fucking way," he said as he pushed past Cecil and into said 'living room.'

As he opened the door, Greg immediately began to sober up. There was no stink of burning flesh in the room, not that he would've noticed even if there had been. Also, the decor had changed considerably. No longer was he in a 16th century mansion. It looked like he'd been transported into an empty operating theatre of the 21st century. The walls and the floor were all one bright white that blended into each other; it was as if there was no start nor end to the room. Oddly, the only furniture was a large, stone open fireplace with a huge Inglenook surround. Beside it was large, brown Chesterfield sofa.

Sitting upon the sofa was a man.

Greg stopped as he entered the room. He immediately dropped to his knees and vomited. Mainly liquid came up. It burned the back of his throat and the inside of his nasal passages as bile and sour booze erupted from his stomach.

The man on the sofa lifted a hand, and, with the smallest of movements, he gestured with delicate fingers.

Cecil helped Greg to his feet and walked him to stand in front of the sofa.

"This is Lord Vandenburgh," Cecil said very quietly.

The Lord was nothing like Greg had imagined. Instead of some crusty old fart in a dusty tweed jacket, he was a handsome man in his mid-fifties. He had a thick mane of black hair with a shock of white at each temple and was dressed in a black suit, black shirt, and black tie. The suit was impeccably tailored in the style of 1920's Prohibition era America.

Greg tried to talk, but nothing came out. It was as if there was no oxygen in his lungs to pass through his throat to create the necessary sounds from his vocal cords. Every time he pushed, the stinging was unbearable. It felt like his throat was lined with acid.

Lord Vandenburgh shook his head slightly. "Don't try to speak," he said softly. Every move he made was minimal. "I know why you are here. Did you bring an item?"

Greg pulled the shoestring from his neck and held it out.

The lord glanced at Cecil, who nodded and took the ring from Greg. He then left the room.

Greg tried to speak again. The lord held a hand up and closed his thumb and forefinger together.

Immediately, Greg's mouth snapped shut.

"You can't speak in here," Lord Vandenburgh told him. "You don't need to. I can *hear* you without the use of primitive language. Welcome to 'the living room.' I know you want to see how I can help you." Lord Vandenburgh snapped his fingers and Cecil returned holding a domed silver platter. He stood beside Greg and lifted the dome to reveal a white rabbit. It was dead. Greg looked at Cecil, who just smiled at him.

Also on the platter was a syringe. Not a modern plastic one, a Victorian glass syringe with brass finger holes and a thick, sewing-machine sized needle.

The lord rolled up a sleeve, patted the inside of his elbow a few times and clenched his fist. He then plucked the syringe from the silver platter with his other hand and plunged the needle with expert dexterity into the vein that bulged like an over-inflated bicycle inner tube. Lord Vandenburgh then filled the vial with thick, dark plasma that more resembled black treacle than blood.

Done, he licked the tiny wound dry of the droplets of blood that oozed out and rolled down his sleeve. He then picked up the deceased rabbit, opened its flaccid eyelid, and injected the contents of the antique syringe into the creature's eye. Vandenburgh placed the syringe back onto the silver platter, and Cecil duly replaced the dome.

The rabbit lay motionless on the lord's lap. He began to stroke the back of its head, gently massaging the spine there. Then he breathed on the animal, gently blowing upon it. His breath spread the soft fur in the same way one would a dandelion clock. Greg saw the paleness of the rabbit's skin beneath.

The lord's strange ritual went on for a few minutes – and then it happened....

The rabbit opened its eyes.

Slowly, it turned its head and looked straight at Greg. The pinkness of the animal's eyes glared at him for a few seconds – they appeared terrified. Then they softened and the rabbit crawled up the lord's chest and settled on his shoulder.

Greg stared incredulously at what he'd just witnessed. The animal was *dead*... And then it wasn't. He tried to speak again. The lord shook his head, which stopped Greg in his tracks.

"You can see what I can do," said Vandenburgh. "You have four hours before sun up to bring her to me. Cecil will help you." With that, the lord snapped his fingers and Greg blacked out.

Lord Vandenburgh smiled to himself, gently lifted the rabbit from his shoulder and nuzzled it to his face.

He then snapped the creature's neck and threw its limp corpse onto the fire.

Greg awoke two hours later freezing cold and without a clue where he was or how he'd got there. Gradually, he remembered what he thought had been a vivid dream.

It was only when he heard Cecil's voice that Greg realised it *wasn't* a dream. He opened his eyes and tried to talk – fully expecting nothing to come out – and was shocked when he heard himself say, "What the fuck? What's happening?"

Greg was scared.

He discovered he was laying on the ground on wet grass. He was covered in mud, his filthy fingers and hands were bloodied, their nails were torn back.

Twisting his head, Greg looked up to see Cecil standing beside him – with Jen's coffin by his side…

"No! No, no, no, no – *fucking no!* This can't be happening! I'm still dreaming… I'm still *fucking dreaming!*"

"No," Cecil told him. This is no dream, Greg. We're going back to the living room now. You have done your duty. It's up to me to get your wife back now. Come along."

Greg couldn't move. He was in a complete state of shock.

Cecil picked up the coffin and hoisted it onto his shoulder like it weighed nothing. He carried Jenny's coffin over to his awaiting Vauxhall Viva estate car, opened the rear door, and slid it in. The coffin hung out of the back a foot or so, and Cecil couldn't close the tailgate. He made his way back to Greg, picked him up with the same ease as he had the coffin, and put him into the back of the car next to the muddy coffin. "You gotta hold onto it to stop it falling out!" he said.

In a daze, Greg just stared into space.

"You listening to me, Boy?" growled Cecil sternly. "Look at me, Boy!" He slapped Greg hard across the face to get his point home.

Greg did as he was told and held onto the box that contained the deceased love of his life.

"We've only got an hour left before the sun comes up for the lord to do his work," Cecil told Greg as he drove the Viva away from the cemetery.

It was a thirty-five-minute drive back to Hockham Hall. By the time they got to the portcullis doorway, the first glow of sunrise was coming up from the mists of the stately home's grounds as the sun's warming rays evaporated the morning dew.

Greg staggered after Cecil in a daze as the man carried Jen's coffin effortlessly through the house and into the living room.

As he followed Cecil into the stark blanket of white, Greg noted it had changed slightly: The fireplace was still there, blazing away, the dark brown chesterfield was where he remembered it from before – but there was now a small, marble altar in the middle of the room. It had a step leading up to it. The altar was surrounded by four oak church pews, all arranged in a square around it. Each pew seated four people, all of whom wore white suits.

At each of the altar's corners stood a young boy of 7 or 8 robed in white. Each one held a white, pink-eyed rabbit just like the one Lord Vandenburgh had resurrected. Every rabbit's fur was matted with blood.

As Greg walked into the living room, he realised he couldn't speak again. He also noticed no one appeared to be breathing. They all smiled at Greg as he walked toward the altar.

At the altar's step stood Lord Vandenburgh. Like the rest of the congregation, he was dressed in a smart, white tuxedo. In one hand was the syringe, once again filled with dark, thick blood.

Cecil placed Jen's coffin on the top of the altar and pulled off its lid like it was nothing more substantial than the top of a shoe box. The lord waved his free hand to Greg to call him over.

Greg moved as if someone else was working him. He looked at his wife's corpse in the coffin and began to silently cry. As he did so, the congregation began to hum a continuous, low note that made the room throb gently.

Lord Vandenburgh stepped up to the coffin, opened Jen's eyelid and injected the dark fluid into her cornea.

Greg opened his mouth to scream but nothing came out.

The lord began gently blowing on Jen's face. He placed the wedding ring Greg had given to him back on her finger. He leant in and softly kissed her pale lips, whispering, "I do."

The humming stopped.

Greg stepped forward to try stopping Vandenburgh by pulling him away. But, with his lips still on the corpse, Lord Vandenburgh held up one finger and Greg stopped in his tracks – his own body just refused to move.

"She is no longer yours!" Lord Vandenburgh waved his hand and Greg was flung by some brutal, invisible force. He hovered, splayed in front of the Inglenook fireplace, suspended in the air, silently screaming as the fire blackened and burnt the flesh from his back and legs and his hair caught fire.

The lord smiled as Greg's once-dead wife opened her eyes and slowly sat up in the white silk-lined coffin.

"It is time to feast, my love. You must be hungry after your fast."

Jenny climbed from the coffin and took the lord's hand. He led her away from the altar and across the living room to the burning, crackling body of Greg – her *first* husband. Kneeling down, she began to peel away the cooked meat from his thighs with her fingers and gorged hungrily upon it.

Cecil brought over the silver platter and a carving knife. Jenny then proceeded to slice away the scorched, sizzling meat from Greg's bones. She placed each morsel with great care upon the tray as he silently screamed.

And still Greg's body cooked; the sinews at the back of his legs tightened from the heat and his skin became crisp and blackened like that of a suckling pig.

Lord Vandenburgh passed the delicacy around the congregation, had all formed a queue to receive their unholy communion. The lord handed out Greg's roasted flesh piece by piece, placing a mouthful of the succulent meat into the unnaturally wide, gaping holes in the faces of each of the hungry followers. Their jaws seemed to dislocate and drop low until they rested upon their chins like a blue whale sieving for plankton.

It took just an hour for Greg's entire body to be consumed. Lord Vandenburgh stood in front of the fire next to Greg's suspended bones and watched the small boys pick the corpse dry of any scraps of remaining flesh.

He looked at Jenny, who stood over by the altar. "Do you think he knew about us?" the lord asked his new bride.

"Not a fucking chance," replied Jenny as her first husband's cooked juices ran down her chin.

Pussy Cat Pussy Cat, Where Have You Been?

I am in mourning.
We are in mourning.
Our queen has died.
Our queen is dead.

She gave her life for our service. To lead her subjects for so long. She didn't ask for it – she was *born* into it in just the same was I was born into my position amongst the millions of nobodies. For so many years, she served us. That's what we are told. That's what we are forced to believe.

But it's not true.

We served *her.* All of us. Not one of us was ever given the chance to keep what we worked for. Everything we earned, we gave to the hierarchy, and we were allowed to keep just enough to keep us alive.

The only reason we are kept alive is to work to keep the aristocracy alive. She got fat from our work, she fed from us; we have given her everything. The working class have no idea what it's like to be royalty. We can only imagine what such a privileged life could be, in which *everything* is handed to you on a platter, where you want for nothing, and all you have to do is reproduce to bring another heir into the world. You could have as many progenies as your body can churn out if you wanted – your whole purpose is to just eat, get fat, and procreate to keep the lineage alive. It's your single, sole reason to be alive.

Look down on we workers. Our lives mean nothing. All that matters is the royal family survives. And all we can do is look on in envy and toil every day until we die.

Incidentally, the death of our queen also coincided with the death of the human queen, Elizabeth II.

Still, life goes on – I've gotta get back to making honey now.

The queen is dead – long live the king!

Sorry, I meant *queen*.

The Curse of Draclia

I'm bored.

I'm so *bloody* bored!

Well, there's no wonder, is there? I'm nearly a thousand years old, and there's not a lot I haven't done.

I'm not an animal lover. I'm not a human lover. When I say I'm not a human lover, I don't *really* mean that. After all, I've made love to humans. What I do mean is that I'm not a lover *of* them – I need them to survive, just for food, maybe entertainment on occasion, but I don't *like* them. And, as I say, I don't like animals, particularly dogs. I *hate* dogs. I mean, I really *fucking hate* them.

I don't remember who my father was. Not my real father, anyway. My *creator* is something altogether different. Or, I should say *was*? He's dead now – I killed him. Not all that long ago, really.

I hadn't seen the man who made me how I am for over 600 hundred years. Let me tell you how this all came about....

The last time I saw my creator, before I killed him, was back in the dark ages. It was during the first English black death plague in Weymouth, Dorset in 1348. The disease originated in Mongolia a few years beforehand and, by 1350, had decimated 200 million of the blood sacks they call *humans*.

You can forget 1665: That plague was like a mild case of the measles in comparison to what went down in 1350! It was designed, made, concocted, administered – whatever you want call it – by my creator's hand (or claw, hoof, or whatever appendages he had at that time, for he took on so many forms.) He created everlasting life within me, and created countless death scenarios for the *sapiens*, but he wasn't much of a father to me.

I mean, he couldn't even say my name properly. He *named* me, and yet couldn't pronounce my name! *Draclia*, he'd call me.

Fucking *Draclia*!

So… I cut his fucking head off.

He'd written me off centuries before. I'd gone through all the stages of trying everything for food – from old men whose blood was thick, coarse, dark, viscous, and heavy with iron to tiny babies. They were my favourite; reminded me of a wonderful taste from when I was human. As a boy, I would find wild raspberries, fill my mouth, and let the blood-red juice run down my throat as I chewed them. Babies tasted the same to me, but they held no more than a pint of the sweet nectar. It was not even enough for an early evening snack. I tried feeding upon animals during the plague in order to avoid catching the disease from sickly people. I kept away from rats, of course, as they were the main instigators of the plague, and cats were a waste of time. The taste was fine, but the scratches were painful. I hated dogs – not only were they stupid, they smelled bad. Their fetid, shit-stained hair matted around their necks smelled to me like the remnants of a goat's dead arse. However, a good-sized horse could give me my fill in one sitting.

However, the best of the bunch – babies aside – were virgins. Sadly, they got harder to find, and were younger all the time. But, oh, the taste of a virgin's plasma was so sweetly sublime for me.

That was until I accidentally drank infected blood from the neck of a virgin. They always tasted sweeter, so I knew she was infected with something the second I tasted her blood. What I didn't know was she had the disease with so many names: 'the blue sickness,' ' the pest,' 'the great mortality,' 'the bubo.'

I knew within a couple of days I'd caught it when I started to get pus-filled boils under my armpits, on my neck, and in my hair. The virgin I'd fed from had no visible lesions on her neck, so she must've had them hidden away somewhere. She'd looked clean to me, and I was *always* meticulous about who I drank from. In the end, I'd become sloppy – weakened by the increasingly difficult challenge of keeping to clean bodies.

I'd spent some time on the fishing boats, moving silently from vessel to vessel. They rarely ventured ashore as they chose the safety of the sea rather than risk being amongst the dying on land. It did mean I fasted for days, even weeks, at a time. Once I'd wiped out the small crew, a boat would be at the mercy of the waves, and I would have to wait until another one found it afloat with only one crew member left on board – me. The crew of the new boat would save me from what they considered a certain death – having unwittingly just created their own….

I was once alone at sea for so long I even tried fish blood. It made me terribly sick, like my insides were filled with rancid bile, as soon as the cold, salty blood hit my stomach. It was then I knew I had to return to shore and take my chances.

So, I headed to Ireland in the hope that the death hadn't reached there. It was then I got the blue sickness. Obviously, it was never gonna kill me, but it made me feel like I *wanted* to be dead. The disease ravaged my body, damaged every cell, every atom of my being, but still I lived. It was strange at first, since I hadn't felt any weakness in my body for hundreds of years.

It made me feel… *human*.

The symptoms were slow to begin… just a chill….

A CHILL?!

God, I'd forgotten what that was!

Then came the fever, coughing – that incessant coughing – as the virus crawled into my lungs and made a home there.

On the few occasions I did try to feed, I would search and search for someone clean, someone living alone, someone miles away from any other humans. Invariably, the second I took a drop of their precious fluid, my body rejected it. The abdominal cramps I endured as I ingested the blood forced it straight back out. I coughed up thick, red clots I could ill afford to waste. My eyes bled, my fingers and toes turned black, my hair fell out, and yet still I lived.

All that time, *he* was watching. I could feel him everywhere because he *was* everywhere. I could almost hear him laughing at me. Offering no help, he just watched me suffer. I knew he could've stepped in at any moment, but he didn't.

Still, I prayed to him. I actually got down on my knees and prayed for his help, but none came. Then my prayers changed: I prayed to die. Of course, I couldn't – not the way humans died of the pestilence. Nonetheless, I died inside.

I used to be strong, invincible, and – even if I say so myself – fucking *handsome*. But, with the ravages of the disease, I became nothing more than a living corpse. Unable to feed, unable to live my *abnormal* life, I had no strength to even take my own life – and God knows I *tried*. I was so weak, I couldn't even slide a wooden shard through my heart.

I recall once sitting in the corner of an old, deserted remnant of a barn on the outskirts of Dublin. I know you're asking yourself why didn't I just wait till the Sun came up, but the honest answer is I was *scared*. I'd contemplated doing just that for months, and decided that night was going to be my last. I crawled out of that old barn and lay there for the morning Sun to take my dying soul. I knew my father could see me, but still he didn't come.

However, something else did.

It was something that changed my undead existence forever.

As I lay there in the fractured moonlight from a brewing storm, weaker than anything I had ever killed, I could do nothing to stop the attack on me. It was swift, unrelenting, and ferocious. At first, I was grateful for the pain I felt as razor-sharp claws slashed across my chest like a scythe. They opened me up, my innards exposed to the cool night air. I was bleeding out, but I knew I wouldn't die.

I felt its teeth sink deep into my neck like hot blades through silk, rupturing my artery there. I bled some more, but I knew I wouldn't die – not until that giant yellow star would take my godless soul.

I remember the sensation of my assailant licking at the wounds in my chest, and then suckling on my neck wound. It was taking the last drops of my undead blood, lapping at it like a kitten at a bowl of warm milk.

I knew I wouldn't die.

When, at last, I heard it creep away into the last few hours of the night, I waited to die.

He watched me.

Even as he watched me bleeding out, he did nothing. He just watched me the way he watches everyone and does nothing.

He just waits.

Closing my eyes, I waited for the sweet release of death. Weakened by the attack upon my diseased body, I passed out. In those last few seconds of consciousness, something deep inside me wanted to live. It was that inbuilt instinct possessed by every living creature to fight to survive. How could that be, when I hadn't been alive for so long?

I began to feel regret as I lay there. Not for what I'd done, not for the lives I'd taken, but for not *really* living.

Then, all I felt was numbing blackness and the rain from the encroaching storm splashing my face.

And then I was gone.

***

I woke up a few hours later with a strange sensation all over my body. I felt no more pain, the wounds in my chest were healed, and the gaping hole in my neck had closed up. I was covered in what was left of my own blood; it had coagulated and dried over my face, my neck, my whole body in fact, but I was warm….

WARM!

I hadn't been warm in centuries. What had happened to me? I tried to open my eyes but could not. I wiped away the caked blood from them and tried once more. The light was blinding. Where was the light and heat coming from?

I pulled myself across the dirt and back into the barn to get away from the heat. Once safely inside, I peeked through the slats in the wood of the barn and saw the heat and light source – it was the Sun.

Why hadn't I died?

I gingerly tested the sunlight by sticking my hand out into it. Scared, I kept my body hidden behind the barn door. Daring the exposure for only a split second, I chanced longer and longer intervals. I fully expected each single photon of sunlight to sear its way through my hand. Instead, my fingers had returned to a normal pinkish hue.

Putting a hand to my chest, I felt my heartbeat and the gentle rise and fall of my own breathing.

I was *alive*.

I stepped out from behind the barn's door and drowned myself in the warm, bright sunlight, basking in it like a sunflower. I felt its power soaking into my skin, healing me. I was *human* again.

There was a water trough beside me. I plunged my hands in and washed away the dried blood. I then immersed my head to clear the dirt and mud from my face and what was left of my hair. As I emerged from the water, I ran my hands over my head to find no more protruding pustules of filth upon my flaking skull. Instead, there was hair, and lots of it! Curious, I looked into the rippling water. As the tiny waves settled, there was my reflection: I was *me*. I was me from hundreds of years ago. I was fucking handsome again!

I drank greedily from the trough. I was drinking *water*! I hadn't tasted it for so long, and it was sweeter than any baby's blood I'd ever drunk as a vampire. I drank my fill. It felt *clean*. I felt cleansed.

HOW?

HOW DID THIS HAPPEN?!

I knew he was watching. I knew he had all the answers, but still he remained in the shadows, just the way he always did. I didn't have to wait too long for the answer to find me, though.

I stayed in the sun all day. I felt born again, like the virgin. And, as the sun started to wane, I felt another familiar, yet *strange,* sensation. It came from my stomach – I was *hungry*. It was a different hunger than before, though. It was hunger not for blood, but for food, real food, *meat*.

I *craved* meat.

Once the night was in full bloom, I decided to go hunting. There were plenty of farms in the nearby area, and I reckoned I could at least find a few chickens if wild rabbits or squirrels were scarce.

I set off under cover of the full blackness of night with a small, rusty hatchet I'd found in the barn. I made my way across several fields and headed towards a dim light in the distance. As I got closer to the light, I felt the pain building inside my stomach again. It was *different*, sharper, more intense.

The pain built up gradually from a series of short stabs in the pit of my guts to my stomach acid turning into what felt like a cauldron of boiling oil. At once, I felt every bone in my body crack and split as they grew and mutated to stab through my flesh. Then, my skin peeled away like that of a rotting carcass and my skull felt like it was about to explode.

The field in front lit up before me – the moon was showing me the way as it instructed every cell in my body to rearrange my DNA and change me into something altogether different.

And change I did.

For the next 600 years, I lived my life as a lycanthrope. I was a *werewolf,* which was horribly ironic. As I said earlier, I fucking hate dogs, and yet he watched and did nothing as his only son became a fucking dog!

He avoided me after that – like the plague.

***

I didn't see him again 'til 1973. He was always somewhere around. I could feel him. Always, but I never saw him.

He was at the London premier of *The Exorcist*.

I saw him.

He'd always loved mixing with the dark side of Hollywood. The underworld of satanism that permeated Tinseltown amused him. He knew they were just playing at it, that they wouldn't know *real* evil if it came at them and introduced itself through their arseholes.

But *he* did.

Unfortunately for him, though, it couldn't save him from his prodigal son.

I hadn't seen my creator in over 600 years, and yet there he was. He was not hiding in the shadows as you'd imagine the Dark One would. No, there he was, in plain sight. As the saying goes, 'speak of the Devil and he's sure to appear.' I was sure he'd call me Draclia just to wind me up. He always did know how to push my buttons.

We were at the movie's after party at the Dorchester. I was a guest of William Friedkin, having met the director a few years previously when he was still in the early stages of researching the movie. I was the go-to guy for anything in the weirding world, and had built up a reputation for owning the best occultist book shop in London. The shop was in Soho, which meant plenty of food and entertainment for me, plus easy pickings amongst lowlifes and people no one really cared about anymore.

He was there, making a scene, holding court. He could mingle as himself with his talons, cloven hooves, forked tail – the full Monty – and have everyone compliment him on his perfect choice of costume.

"How fitting."

"Oh, you devil!"

"Feeling horny*?"*

That night, he spread his vile seed with the ones who followed him. Not just once, but with many – *legion*, in fact. He left the room after he'd made the many, and I followed him out into the night.

To the back of the dimly lit loading bay behind the hotel. He crossed the road and walked into Hyde Park. I tailed him quietly, and, as he reached the darkness beneath the trees, he turned and smiled at me. His eyes were as clear and red as rubies, his ivory teeth gleaming as his lips curled up in a sinister smile.

"Draclia. My son. It's been a while. What have you been up to?"

I began to answer him. "Well –"

He waved his hand dismissively and said, "It's not important. In 9 months, you're going to have a brother. Well, a few brothers, actually. You've been a bitter disappointment to me, Draclia, so I thought I'd make some new offspring. Hopefully, they'll turn out to be better than you. You understand, don't you? I mean, whoever heard of a werewolf called *Draclia*?"

"My name… is *Dracula*," I snarled. Then, with one swipe of my long, sharp claws, I took his head clean off.

I watched, amused, as my creator's head rolled in a crude semicircle in the grass and stopped at my feet. Rocking gently from side to side, it settled face-up. His eyes slowly opened, his mouth curled up into that smile of his, and he said, "Who the Hell wants to go to Heaven anyway?!"

Then he disappeared as if he'd never existed.

Velvet Elvis

Chapter 1
Long Live the King

Oh fuck.

He's here again. I can hear him coming. Why the fuck doesn't he just leave me alone?

I can't tell anyone – who would believe me? If someone told me the same tale, I wouldn't believe them, either…

Ask yourself this:

If someone said to you Elvis Presley came to visit them every night – not in real life, but in their brain – and he takes control of their body to make them do the most God-awful things, would you believe them?

Would you fuck?!

Of course, you wouldn't. But it's true! It happens to me – a *lot*. Some of you out there reading this may even be jealous of me. Maybe you wish it could happen to you?

Well, let me tell you something. You don't want to wish for that because when he comes – and he's coming, he's getting closer now – it's really, *really* bad.

I see him. I hear him just as I'm hearing him now. First of all, I hear him singing. It's not like listening to the King on the radio or on a record, though. I hear his voice in my head as clear as if he was in the room with me. And, it's never the same song each time. It's always one of his big hits, though. Sometimes it's a cover of someone else's song, but always a song Elvis had recorded and 'made his own.'

When he gets closer, it's *all* I can hear. Then I see him in the distance. He's walking towards me, and there's nothing I can do. If I turn away from him in my mind, Elvis is still walking towards me. I can never lose him. To me, it's almost like he's in heaven, jumping from cloud to cloud, using each one as a stepping stone. As he gets closer to me, I lose myself, become *him*, and start to do his bidding.

The song is always a herald, Elvis' way of letting me know he's coming....

I don't know why, but he's never fat in my mind. He's never that sad, fat Elvis in the rhinestone jumpsuits, heeled Cuban boots, dodgy-framed sunglasses, and stupid cape. Oh, no, *my* Elvis would never be seen dead like that. When he comes to me, he's the '68 Comeback Special Elvis: lean, slick, and snake-hipped. Nothing at all like the lumbering hippo we all remember just before he died.

Yet, he's not wearing the black leathers he wore for that comeback. No, he's wearing the softest, red velvet suit, and he's like a fucking Greek god in my mind.

When he's here, he offers me a chair in my head upon which to sit. From there, I must observe everything he says and does. I'm completely helpless, *powerless* to stop him.

I guess I should be grateful when Elvis visits me. When he's here, I feel young again, my body no longer aches – being 81, *everything* hurts – and I don't need my walking frame. I also straighten up, my spine no longer curves, my toes are straight, and my knees no longer bow.

When Elvis arrives, the first thing he does is to pull out the catheter from what used to be my splendid penis. It's just a worn-away nubbin now, although it's restored to its former glory in his presence. Elvis pulls that plastic tube out and throws the accompanying bag strapped to my leg into the nearest bin.

And then we piss.

Elvis and me piss like I did when I was 25, and I *feel* my prostate gland shrink back to how it was before the cancer grew in it. We piss for what seems like forever, and I get an erection – I haven't had one of those for nearly 15 years! – and it's like that for the duration. Our pissing is always to the same song: Elvis singing *Burning Love*.

Oh, the wonderful irony!

It all started about 6 months ago when my daughter, Lisa Marie, said I wasn't able to look after myself anymore. What the fuck did she know? I was fine – out-of-date food is never *really* out of date. I'd lived through the fucking war, for God's sake! I was evacuated to Beccles in Suffolk as a kid and lived on fucking horse meat. So, leaving the stove on, falling asleep, and letting the eggs boil dry was nothing. I'd have smelled the burning eventually and woken up. But no, the last straw for her was the *fall*.

Everybody fucking falls over!

It's *gravity*, for fuck's sake!

So, I was dumped in here. Graceland's Home for the Elderly – in fucking *Tilbury*. Not exactly Memphis, is it?

"You'll like it here, Dad," Lisa Marie told me. "It's called 'Gracelands.' That's where Elvis lived. You and Mum loved Elvis, didn't you?!"

"Fuck off," I snapped. "I *hated* him. That was your mum, and she's been gone 15 years now."

"Well, she's in a better place now," my daughter patronised me.

"Ha!" I grumbled. "*Anywhere* is better than this fucking place. Don't let the door slam you on the arse on the way out."

She left.

I've not seen my darling daughter since. Well, she's not getting her inheritance now, that's one thing for sure.

There's 126 of us here. Well, there was until *he* arrived: the King. He simply turned up one night at about 2 o'clock in the morning. I awoke to him singing *American Trilogy*. At first, I thought it was one of the other 'inmates.' I call us that 'cos that's what we are: We have no freedom, we're told when to get up, when to eat, when to go to bed, when to shit – it truly is like a bloody concentration camp in here!

So, I just thought one of the dried-up, ugly old bints down the corridor had turned on a radio to help them sleep. I enjoyed it at first, but then I realised it was in my head. Then I saw him, as clear as anything. Elvis looked me dead in the eye, curled his lip, and said, "Sit back, relax, enjoy the trip."

I sat down for the first time in that metaphysical chair in my mind, and Elvis finished up singing *Trilogy*. His voice was better than ever.

Standing up, I walked over to the mirror on the wall and glanced into it. I didn't see *me*, I saw Elvis. He smiled. I don't know if he was actually smiling at me or to himself. He said, "Looking good, boy, looking good. TCB – taking care o' business."

As we left my room, he said, "This room smells, man. It smells of *old man*. It smells of ass – it smells of old man's ass!"

We walked along the corridor past a half dozen or so doors. Elvis walked just the way I'd seen him in the documentaries I'd watched with Doreen, with that unmistakable, cocky swagger.

Doreen and me had been married 35 years, and she was bloody *obsessed* with bloody Elvis. I had to watch *everything* about the man, sit through his stupid films, listen to every song he ever recorded. It got right on my tits, I can tell you. I was *actually* glad the fat fuck died when he did.

When Elvis passed on, Doreen made a shrine to him in our bathroom: Elvis towels, Elvis bath mat, Elvis flannel, an Elvis toilet seat that played *Love*

Me Tender when you sat on it. Even our bloody Soap On A Rope had his fucking face on it! I washed my arse as much as I could with that soap and flannel, but I still had to watch everything he ever did. And, that night when he appeared, it all came back to me.

Elvis walked like he was flanked by a dozen security guards as he made his way to the stage at Caesar's Palace in Vegas. He was all ready to sing to his adoring, sycophantic fans, who all screamed and held out their hands as he walked by. They all wanted to touch Elvis as if he was some modern-day Jesus. I figured those dumb women thought that by just one touch, he would heal all the wrongs in their lives.

The King?

Well, as far as I was concerned, Elvis was no king to me – he was a fucking fraud. And yet, there he was – right inside my head.

We stopped outside room 17 and stared at the door for a couple of minutes. We both read the name written in chalk on the small blackboard hanging on the door. There was no permanence to the occupancies of the rooms at Gracelands because we were all busy getting to the end. As we did so, we all grew ever-more bitter and twisted with our un-lived lives, regretted the things we never did, and resented all the people we blamed for stopping us living our dreams.

"Here," Elvis said in his baritone, southern drawl. "This is the one." He licked the palm of my hand and slicked my hair back. I felt a kiss curl fall against my forehead. How could I possibly feel that when I'd lost most of my hair in my mid-40's? Nonetheless, I felt the flop of that quiff land squarely on my brow.

Elvis whispered the name on the board, "Jennie Acaster. I'm a'comin, honey. Just you hold on, now."

We opened the door and went in.

All Gracelands' rooms were identical. We all had the same mirror in the exact same position and height, a pale brown chest of drawers, a single bed, and an uncomfortable armchair. It was like living in a down-market Travelodge. As we walked past Jennie's mirror, we glanced into it. All I saw was Elvis in his red velvet suit, but Jennie would only see the real me standing there in my baggy old pants.

The bedside lamp was on, but Jennie was asleep. Elvis and I stood by the bed and gently shook her 'til her puffy eyes opened and she was greeted by the sight of me in my pants – that ancient pair of blood and piss-stained pajama bottoms. The stains were from the trauma of the catheter being ripped from my pathetic old penis, which was still kind of erect. The waistband of my pants was partly hidden by my fat belly hanging over its top, but Jennie could see I was aroused.

She smiled. It was the first time I'd seen the old hag smile in the 6 months I'd been at the home.

"Ooh," she purred as she sat up in bed. She put her glasses on and stared at my appendage. "I think I know what you're after! Feeling a bit fruity, are you, Dennis?"

"Shut up, lady," said Elvis. "I'm not Dennis. I'm the King. I'm Velvet Elvis."

"Oh." Jennie grinned. "You fancy a bit of role playing, do you? Well, I'll be Marilyn Monroe. You wanna titty dance?" She began unbuttoning her white flannel nightgown.

"I said shuddup," barked Elvis. "I don' wanna see them damn ugly udders. I'm here TCB – taking care o'bizness. I know what you did, darlin'. I know about that kid you ran over and left for dead. I know what you did, Jennie Acaster. That kiddie died all on his own that night, and his mamma never knew what happened and died of a broken heart. You gonna pay, old lady. We all gotta pay in the end, an' I'm here to collect."

The smile on Jennie's face disappeared. "How do you know about that?" she spat.

Elvis curled his lip. "Ah know everythin', little lady. I'm Velvet Elvis."

"It was an *accident*," Jennie insisted. "I'd had a drink or two. It was my first date, my first kiss. I just didn't see the kid. He just came out of nowhere. He had no lights on his bike… I was just –"

"Ah' know, honey," said Elvis. "Ah know. But it's time to pay." So saying, Elvis slipped a pillow from behind her head and sang to Jennie as he pushed it down firmly into her face.

"Oh, I wish I was in the land of cotton… old things, they're not forgotten… look away, look away… look away… Dixieland…."

Jennie's legs kicked out wildly, her back arching as she desperately tried to find air at the sides of the pillow.

But he – *I* – kept on pushing and he – *I* – kept on singing.

"Glory, glory, hallelujah… glory, glory, hallelujah… glory, glory, hallelujah… His truth is marching on…."

The old woman was 87, but fuck, she was strong. Her bony hands punched at me from behind the antiallergenic pillow, her nails scratched deep into my hands and arms.

But Velvet Elvis kept on singing over her muffled screams.

"Hush, little baby… don't you cry…. you know your daddy is bound to die…. but all my trials Lord, will soon be over…."

Elvis took a deep breath and made ready to belt out the last refrain of *glory, glory hallelujahs*, but stopped when he realised Jennie wasn't struggling anymore.

We stood up and lifted up the old woman's head to place the pillow back behind her limp neck. We laid Jennie Acaster in a position that looked like she'd died peacefully in her sleep, straightened the bed sheets, and went back into the dark hallway. Just before we left Jennie's room, Elvis looked in the mirror, winked at me, and said, "Ladies and gentlemen... Velvet Elvis has left the building."

I woke up the next morning to a bed soaking-wet from my own piss and a hangover like someone had been dynamiting my brain.

Then, I remembered *everything*.

Looking down at my hands and arms, I saw the scratches Jennie had made were gone. *Oh, thank fuck for that*, I thought. *It must've been a dream*. I lay back onto the cold wetness of the bed and breathed a sigh of relief.

Shortly afterwards, I buzzed for a care assistant to come and put in a new catheter and change my sheets. I buzzed and I buzzed for nearly an hour, but no one came.

So, I started shouting.

"Can I get some fucking service here?! I'm lying in a bed of piss! It's so fucking wet, there's a bloody rainbow hanging over me!"

The door to my room opened sharply.Claire, one of the nursing assistants, popped her head round.

Shhhhh, you rude old man," she hissed. "Have some respect, will you? Jennie passed away last night. I'll be with you as soon as I can!"

Chapter 2.
The Second Coming.

A week later, Elvis was back.

I'd hoped Jennie had been his one and only appearance at the Gracelands venue, but no chance.

I hadn't slept much at all since his last visit. I was exhausted, just drifting in and out of consciousness all hours of the day, petrified he might return.

And return he did.

It was Friday night. I lay there in my bed trying not to fall asleep in case that was how he found his way into my mind. I'd seen all those old *Nightmare on Elm Street* films, where Freddie Kruger attacked teenagers in their dreams, so figured it was a safe strategy.

No such luck.

I was still awake at 4 in the morning when I heard him. Distant at first, his voice was faint, but there was no mistaking it. I wasn't hallucinating – Velvet Elvis was coming.

He sang *Are You Lonesome Tonight*; his melodious voice in my head growing louder and louder.

Then I saw him.

My red-velvet tormentor was back. He stood there in front of me and pointed to the chair in my mind. Obediently, I sat down in it. Elvis curled that famous lip of his and said, "It's sho' time, old man. Enjoy the ride."

He yanked the tube out of my withered old knob and struck his stage pose: down on one knee and pointing to a nonexistent audience. As we stood, Elvis played air guitar on the plastic catheter tube like it was a bizarre, single-stringed Fender. As he did so, he sang, *"A little less conversation, a little more action, please."*

We walked to my mirror and paused. Elvis rolled up his sleeves and showed me the long, white scars from the scratches Jennie had left on his arms. "She was a wild one!" he laughed.

Standing back from the mirror, we faced the other way. Elvis placed his hands on his hips, stood with his legs apart, spun around on one heel, and said, "Draw." He mimed pulling a pistol from invisible holsters and firing them. Elvis blew the imaginary smoke from the tips of his index fingers and said, "Come on, boy. We got work to do."

We made our way up to room 62. There, the name chalked on the blackboard was Frank Thompson.

"This is th' guy," Elvis said. "Let's go, compadre."

We found Frank sitting in his high-winged Sherlock Holmes chair. He had an oxygen mask over his mouth and nose – he never slept in the bed because he couldn't lay on his back. Lung cancer and emphysema had put paid to that years ago, and Frank used to choke every night, hacking his way all through the dark hours. In the end, he just gave up and spent all day and all night in that chair.

The alarm clock was the only light in the room. Glowing an eerie LED red, it showed the time to be 4.20 a.m.

We switched on Frank's bedside lamp and sat on the edge of his bed. The poor old bastard had the full set: colon cancer, diabetes, cataracts, heart disease, the lot.

Frank opened his eyes. He squinted at us. "Dennis? Is that you, Dennis? What you want at this time of –"

"Shut your mouth, ol' man. I ain't Dennis," we interrupted him. "I'm Velvet Elvis, and it's time to pay your dues. I know what you did. I know what you did to that old blind man when you were 17. I know you followed him home from the shops... he was a kind ol' man who wouldn't hurt nuthin' or no one. But you, Frank, you *know* what you did."

Frank looked petrified. A single tear ran down his cheek. "I'm sorry," he said through the clear plastic mask.

"Damn right, you're sorry," said Elvis. "You killed that wonderful old man and his dog. And for what? A few measly bucks so you could buy your fuckin' drugs!"

"I'm so sorry, Dennis," blubbed Frank. "I was just a kid. I was on the street. I didn't know what I was doing –"

"Shut the fuck up!" snapped Elvis. "I already told you – I *ain't* Dennis! I'm Velvet Elvis, an' it's time for retribution. You gotta pay for what ya did, ol' timer. So, sit back and close your eyes. This won't take long."

Resigned to his fate, Frank slumped back into the chair. He kept his eyes open and watched me, and so did I....

I watched my hands open his bedside drawer and take out a small leather pouch. I saw myself unzip the bag and take out a plastic, disposable syringe. I pierced the bottle of insulin with the needle, drew back the plunger, and filled the syringe with the clear liquid; I drew up every last drop in that vial.

"This won't hurt," said Elvis as I watched myself inject the insulin overdose into Frank's arm. We began to sing quietly as Frank gently closed his eyes for the final time.

"I wrote a letter to the postman, he put it in his sack. Bright early next morning, he brought my letter back... She wrote upon it, return to sender, address unknown, no such number, no such zone...."

We sat and watched Frank fall into a diabetic coma, safe in the knowledge he'd be dead before too long.

"He'll be pushin' up daisies by sun up," said Elvis. "Now you gotta get some sleep, ol' boy. 'Cos we got more work to do!"

Turning off Frank's bedside lamp, Velvet Elvis and me left Frank's room. The alarm clock glowed 4.30 a.m.

Chapter 3
Return Bookings

The visits escalated.

Velvet Elvis would come to me at least twice a week, sometimes more, but the pattern remained the same.

After Jennie and Frank, there was Peter in room 89 – we turned off his ventilator to the tune of *Blue Moon of Kentucky*. There was Vera in room 47, snuffed out by asphyxiation using a soft toy her granddaughter had given her to keep her company. We serenaded her final moments with *Let Me Be Your Teddy Bear*.

Elvis thought that was funny.

The list went on and on. Elvis' visits became more and more frequent. Sammi, room 51, late night bath – electrocuted by his radio falling in. The last song he heard was *Jailhouse Rock*.

There was Patricia in room 27, dispatched courtesy of anaphylactic shock. The nasty old bird had a severe nut allergy – broadcast for all to see on a curled, yellow Post-It above her bed. We forced a bar of Cadbury's Fruit and Nut into her fat face while singing *A Whole Lotta Livin' To Do*. Again, Elvis thought he was being hilarious.

Eventually, he came every night, and everybody thought the home was cursed. With so many people dying, the staff were having sweepstakes on who was gonna be next. Of course, I knew it was never gonna be me, and the strange thing was that I was getting to like it. I'd started to enjoy myself and actually looked forward to Velvet Elvis's nightly visits.

But then it stopped.

The moment I got enjoyment from what me and Elvis were doing, it stopped as abruptly as it had started.

That was 6 weeks ago.

Chapter 4
A Curtain Call.

Nobody has died in the past 6 weeks.

I know that stops tonight.

I just woke up because someone switched my bedside light on. There, standing beside my bed is Gordon Wentworth. The old git is well into his 90s.

"What the fuck do you want, Gordon," I grumble at him. "It's 4 in the fucking morning?"

Gordon stares at me blankly for a few seconds before replying. "I'm not Gordon. I'm fuckin' Von Ryan's Express Frank Sinatra, and you done some bad things, old' man. You gonna pay – the Chairman of the Board is here now."

Gordon's wiry old hands – surprisingly strong and steady for a man of such advanced years and Parkinson's – wrap around my throat, and the last thing I hear before my world goes dark is: *"And now, the end is near, and so I face the final –"*

Exit stage right.

Velvet Elvis has really left the building.

ABOUT THE AUTHOR

Joe Pasquale, comedian and author, has continued to delight audiences with his live stand-up tours for over 30 years. Along the way, he's voiced characters for Hollywood movies *Garfield: A Tale of Two Kittens*, *Horton Hears a Who!*, as well as children's television animation: *Frankenstein's Cat*. He also starred in The Muppets' 25th Anniversary show.

Having qualified as a pilot and taking up boxing and running, Joe enhanced his 'action man' credentials by competing in a celebrity edition of *Total Wipeout* against the likes of Fatima Whitbread and Sally Gunnell. He's also achieved the 'most martial arts throws in a minute' on *Guinness World Records Smashed*, spent time in a Costa Rican prison for Virgin One's *The Prisoner X* documentary season, and was shipped off to the jungles of Guyana for the Discovery Channel's *Alone in the Wild* series, where he survived alone with a camera in the depths of the rainforest for 5 days!

Joe has written two collections of short horror stories: *Deadknobs and Doomsticks* – volumes i and ii. *Of Mice and Wolfmen* is his third collection to date, and he is working on his first full-length novel.

www.joepasquale.com

Other HellBound Books available at
www.hellboundbooks.com

The Toilet Zone: Number Two
"Restroom reading at its most terrifying!"

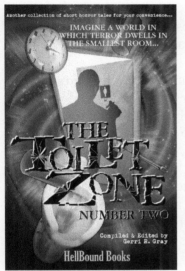

The second in HellBound Books' trilogy of toilet terror – every tale the perfectly calculated length for a visit...

Imagine, if you will, you're traveling through the unknown, hellbound, with no roadmap or stars to guide you. The light fades as you descend into a shadow realm where supernatural terrors make their lair and evil lurks at every turn. Here, dead things don't always stay dead, for this is a world where things that shouldn't be... *are*, and things that should be are not.

In this world, it takes between 2,500 and 4,000 reading words to pay a visit to the smallest, but terrifyingly necessary, room, and stories are written precisely to chill the bones as you wait for nature to make its call.

You open up the book, and one of the 32 tales skulking within its hellish pages chooses you...

It's too late to turn back now. You are about to set foot into another dimension, so best watch out for that signpost up ahead...You've just crossed over into... The Toilet Zone

HellBound Books' Anthology of Splatterpunk

splat·ter·punk
noun
informal
noun: splatterpunk

Definition: "A literary genre characterized by graphically described scenes of an extremely gory nature."

HellBound Books are incredibly proud to present to you horror most raw and visceral, two-dozen suitably graphic, horrific tales of terror designed to churn the stomach and curdle the blood.

This superlative tome is an absolute must for fans of Richard Laymon, Clive Barker, Monica J. O'Rourke, Matt Shaw, Wrath James White and Jack Ketchum – all put to paper by some of the brightest new stars writing in the genre today.

Featuring stories by: Nick Clements, Carlton Herzog, NJ Gallegos, Scotty Milder, Steve Stark, Frederick Pangbourne, Cristalena Fury, Amber Willis, Kenneth Amenn, Erica Summers, Allie Guilderson, Cory Andrews, Andrew P. Weston, Shula Link, Carlton Herzog, DW Milton, Brent Bosworth, JD Fuller, Robert Allen Lupton, C.M. Noel, Julian Grant, Jay Sykes, Phil Williams, and the incomparable James H Longmore.

Madame Gray's Poe-Pourri of Terror

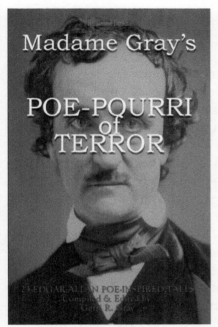

A haunting collection of twenty-three terror-filled tales that pay loving homage to - and capture the very essence of - Edgar Allan Poe.

So, prepare yourself for blood-chilling nightmares as murder, madness, and the supernatural are masterfully blended together to create a delectably wicked potpourri of the macabre.

Featuring exemplary stories of horror from:

R. C. Mulhare, Scot Carpenter, Stephen A. Roddewig, Gerardo Serrano R., Greg Patrick, Drew Nicks, J. Rocky Colavito, Bernardo Villela, James Musgrave, Carlton Herzog, Barbara Jacobson, Guy Riessen, Jane Nightshade, Floyd Mcmillan, Jr., Jeanette Gibson, Bill Camp, J Louis Messina, N.D. Coley, Brett Knepper, Josh Poole, Jameson Grey, and the inimitable Gerri R. Gray

Made in Britain

The very best in all-British horror by British authors!

There is something quite special about this fine collection of tales of terror from the Sceptered Isle, each and every one crafted in the dead of the night by twisted, fevered minds, who have brought crawling and slithering to life the darkest denizens of the blackest shadows to terrify those brave souls amongst you who dare to read...

For your delectation, Dear Reader, we have assembled together between these illustrious covers an array of the finest British authors:
Guy N. Smith, James H Longmore, David Owain Hughes, Kevin J Kennedy, Ross Baxter, C. Bailey-Bacchus, Justin Boote, Munib Haroon, Lex H Jones, Michael Byrne, Lee Franklin, J. C. Michael, Bill Davidson, Andrew J Lucas, Nick Stead, David Turnbull, Michael Chapman, and Richard Farren Barber

Blood and Kisses

"Think of what late greats James Herbert and Richard Laymon may have given birth to had they ever collaborated" - Richard Chizmar

The definitive short story collection from horror author James H Longmore - an eclectic mix of dark horror, bizarro and *Twilight Zone* style tales of the downright disturbing.

Welcome to the long-awaited collection from the acclaimed writer of horror novels *'Pede* and *Tenebrion*; a foreword by Richard Chizmar (co-author of *Gwendy's Button Box* with Stephen King), 18 short stories, 5 flash fiction, and a poem - all skin-crawling, soul-shredding tales of the darkest things that skulk among the night's inky shadows and of the everyday gone horribly awry.

Discover the implication of technology becoming self-aware, enjoy the acquaintance of a charismatic new pastor promising his flock a brand-new place to worship his God, spend a little time in the company of a nice young man who is inexorably caught up in his home town's terrible secret.

Then, there's Cupid's revelation he's never experienced love, we discover that very emotion alive and not so well among the ruins of a post-zombie apocalyptic world, and bear witness to childhood innocence forever destroyed in a distant, war-torn city.

Observe, too any unsavory individual's obsession with the ever-elusive snuff movie, and join an elderly bunch of forgetful sleuths out to solve the mystery of brutal deaths that occur with alarming regularity at their memory care facility.

Now, have you ever considered what may happen should you have the misfortune to bump into your family's doppelgangers on a long, tedious road trip? And, can you even begin to imagine being the doting father who finally realizes the apple of his eye's true identity, or the parents who spend what is left of their crumbling lives waiting by a silent telephone for news of their addict son?

There is more, Dear Reader, much, much more; for within the pages, we have devils, demons and ghosts, lycanthropes, and demi-gods, all rubbing nefarious shoulders with the vilest of Hell's offspring, who have slithered up from the netherworld to doff their caps and wish us all the sweetest of dreams…

**A HellBound Books LLC
Publication 2023**

www.hellboundbooks.com

Printed in the United States of America

Ingram Content Group UK Ltd.
Milton Keynes UK
UKHW012323190623
423717UK00015B/260/J